Stories in My Pocket

Tales Kids Can Tell

Martha Hamilton and Mitch Weiss
Beauty and the Beast Storytellers

Illustrations by Annie Campbell

Fulcrum Publishing
Golden, Colorado

Book design by Deborah Rich

Library of Congress Cataloging-in-Publication Data

Hamilton, Martha.
    Stories in my pocket : tales kids can tell / Martha Hamilton and
  Mitch Weiss ; illustrations by Annie Campbell.
      p. cm.
  Includes bibliographical references and index.
  Summary: Includes thirty stories chiefly from folk
  literature, helpful tips for storytelling, and an overview for the
  adults involved in the activity.
    ISBN 1-55591-957-X (pbk.)
    1. Storytelling—Juvenile literature.   2. Children's stories.
  [1. Storytelling.   2. Folklore.]   I. Weiss, Mitch.   II. Campbell,
  Annie, ill.   III. Title.
  LB1042.H337   1996
  372.6'4—dc20
                         96-12750
                         CIP
                         AC

Printed in the United States of America

0 9 8 7 6 5 4 3 2

Fulcrum Publishing
350 Indiana Street, Suite 350
Golden, Colorado 80401-5093
(800) 992-2908   •   (303) 277-1623

To the memory of my Aunt Lucy Mae Wallace
whose spunk and perseverance
were an inspiration to me

—M. H.

To the memory of my Dad
who cheered me on at every game
and would have done the same at storytelling events,
and whom I thank most of all
for his gifts of wit and humor

—M. W.

For my Mumsey and my Dadsey,
with many thanks
for all your encouragement

—A. C.

Acknowledgments

Thanks to the children with whom we've worked and who have helped to shape these stories over the last sixteen years. Your energy and enthusiasm keep us going. Also to the many teachers who have opened their classrooms to us and given us the support we needed.

We are grateful to Byrd Baylor, Carol Birch, Joe Bruchac, Richard and Judy Dockrey Young, Laurel Hodgden, Robert Munsch, and Diane Wolkstein for their great generosity in allowing their stories to be reprinted; to Kate and Tim Weiss for their help with the poem; to Leah Kaminsky, Emmie Smith, and Daniel Miller for their story web, map, and outline; to Glynn Chesnut who is always there when we need her to type or file or copy something, but who refuses to do ironing; to Marcelle Toor for consulting and advice on illustrators; to Carolyn Abbott, Marty Kaminsky, and June Locke for reading the manuscript and giving many helpful suggestions; to Peter Grossman for his lawyerly advice, always at a good rate; and to Jan Nigro, the master of meter, for his help with the poem.

A special thanks to Annie Campbell for her wonderful drawings that make the stories come alive and for making our fax machine purchase worthwhile; also to Suzanne Barchers for her remarkable ability to come up with instant solutions to problems we agonized over for hours and for all those chats on the telephone. Thank goodness for toll-free numbers.

Finally, thanks to all of our friends on the road who have opened their homes, hearts, and kitchens to us over the past sixteen years, and to our friends in this wonderful community of Ithaca who are always a pleasure to come home to.

Permissions

Permission to reprint the following is gratefully acknowledged:

"Bracelets" was adapted by permission from Carol L. Birch from *Joining In: An Anthology of Audience Participation Stories and How to Tell Them* compiled by Teresa Miller. Cambridge, MA: Yellow Moon, 1988. Permission was also granted by storyteller Diane Wolkstein and the original author Laurel Hodgden. Her story "The Little Girl Who Liked Bracelets," appeared in *School Before Six—A Manual for Nursery School Teachers*. St. Louis: CEMREL Institute, 1974.

"The Beautiful Dream" from *And It Is Still That Way: Legends Told by Arizona Indian Children* by Byrd Baylor. Sante Fe, NM: Trails West Publishing, 1988. (Originally published by Scribners in 1976.) Reprinted by permission of the author.

"How Coyote Was the Moon" from *Keepers of the Earth: Native American Stories and Environmental Activities for Children* by Michael Caduto and Joseph Bruchac. Golden, CO: Fulcrum, 1988. Reprinted by permission of the author.

The Paper Bag Princess by Robert N. Munsch. Illustrated by Michael Martchenko. Toronto: Annick Press, 1980. Distributed by Firefly Books, Scarborough, Canada. Reprinted by permission of the author. No commercial or theatrical performances of this work can be given without prior written permission of the author. This does not include telling by children, teachers, or librarians in school settings.

"Skunnee Wundee and the Stone Giant" from *Favorite Scary Stories of American Children* by Richard and Judy Dockrey Young (August House, 1990). Copyright © 1990 by Richard and Judy Dockrey Young. Reprinted by permission.

Contents

"A Story in My Pocket"   **viii**

Storytelling Tips for Kids   **1**

Introduction   **3**

Choosing a Story to Tell   **5**

Learning Your Story   **6**

Telling Your Story   **12**

Thirty Stories to Tell
With Suggestions on How to Tell Them   **21**

How to Use Our Suggestions for Telling Stories   **23**

Starter Stories   **24**
    The Beautiful Dream *(Native American/Navajo Tribe)*   25
    The Mysterious Box *(Scandinavia)*   28
    The Night the Moon Fell Into the Well *(Turkey)*   31
    The Bundle of Sticks *(Greece/Aesop)*   33
    Who Will Fill the House? *(Latvia, Lithuania)*   35
    Oh, That's Good! No, That's Bad! *(United States)*   37

Next Step Stories   **40**
    The Mouse and the Sausage *(France)*   41
    How Coyote Was the Moon *(Native American/Kalispel Tribe)*   44
    Tilly *(England, Canada, United States)*   47
    The Biggest Lie *(Russia)*   50
    The Biggest Donkey of All *(Armenia, Turkey, Russia)*   53
    Why Crocodile Does Not Eat Hen *(Africa/Bantu)*   56
    The Brave but Foolish Bee *(Greece/Aesop)*   59
    Fox and His Tail *(Mexico, Nicaragua)*   62
    Bat Plays Ball *(Native American/Creek Tribe)*   66
    Do They Play Soccer in Heaven? *(United States)*   70

Contents

Challenging Stories   **74**

    Bracelets *(Laurel Hodgden)*   75

    Skunnee Wundee and the Stone Giant *(Native American/Algonkian Tribes)*   79

    On a Dark and Stormy Night *(United States)*   84

    Clytie *(Greece)*   89

    The Golden Arm *(England)*   93

    The Silversmith and the Rich Man *(Jewish)*   97

    Why Anansi the Spider Has a Small Waist *(West Africa)*   102

    King Midas and the Golden Touch *(Greece)*   106

Most Challenging Stories   **111**

    The Mirror That Caused Trouble *(Korea)*   112

    The Paper Bag Princess *(Robert N. Munsch)*   117

    Who Will Close the Door? *(India)*   122

    The Stonecutter *(Japan)*   127

    Wait Till Whalem-Balem Comes *(United States/African-American)*   132

    Master of All Masters *(England)*   138

Finding Other Stories to Tell   **143**

The Elements of a Good Story for Telling   **144**

More Stories You Can Tell: A Bibliography   **145**

Storytelling Resources   **148**

**Guidelines for Adults
to Help Kids Tell Stories**   **149**

Why Children Should Be Given the Opportunity to Tell Stories   **151**

Fostering Storytelling at Home   **154**

Storytelling in the School, Camp, or Other Group Setting   **156**

How to Teach Kids to Tell Stories   **158**

Where Children Can Tell Stories   **172**

Related Creative Activities   **176**

Good Luck with Your Storytelling Adventures   **178**

Appendix: Story Sources   179

Index   183

A Story in My Pocket

Martha Hamilton and Mitch Weiss
Beauty and the Beast Storytellers

*With a story in my pocket
And a poem on my lips
I'm never tired or bored
When we take our family trips.*

*At a sleep over or camp out,
If my best friend's feeling blue,
At a family reunion,
I spin a tale or two.*

*Ghost tales give the shivers,
Legends weave a spell,
Tall tales give the giggles,
So many kinds to tell.*

*At first I got so scared
My heart would start to pound.
I thought I might forget
Or say it the wrong way 'round.*

*It's fun when listeners smile
To scare them feels so great.
When asked to tell another
I know I just can't wait!*

*No one can take these tales from me
Because they're in my head.
Someday I'll tell them to my kids
As I tuck them into bed.*

Storytelling Tips for Kids

Introduction

You Mean *I* Can Tell Stories?

Perhaps you've seen a storyteller at your school, camp, library, or local park. Unless it was an unusual event, the storyteller was probably an adult. You may have thought, "I wonder if *I* could do that?" Of course you can! Whether you realize it or not, you already are a storyteller! You tell stories all the time—about what happened on the school bus today, the time you got lost, or the great practical joke your dad once played on his brother.

If something really funny happens to you, and then you see a friend, what's the first thing you want to do? Tell about it! Storytelling can be as simple as sitting in your living room and sharing what happened today with a good friend. It can be standing and telling a story in front of a group around a campfire, in a classroom, or on a street corner on a summer's day. Storytelling can be your mom or dad telling you about the day you were born or about something that happened to them when they were kids. And, of course, it can be anyone telling a folktale or myth that has been passed down for thousands of years. These are just a few of the many forms storytelling can take.

Our job for the past sixteen years has been telling stories and teaching kids and adults to tell stories. It's an unusual but very enjoyable way to make a living. After we've taught a group of kids to tell stories, we always have them fill out a form about how they felt at the beginning when they first chose a story, and at the end when they actually told their stories for a group. Many feel the way an eleven-year-old named David did. He wrote, "At first I thought, 'I'll never be able to do this.' I was so worried I might mess up and everyone would laugh at me. But by the time I told my story I had practiced so much that it felt easy. When I saw everyone smiling and clapping, it was a great feeling. Now I think I can do anything!" And a nine-year-old named Jennifer wrote: "I was scared to death. I thought I might forget everything and just stand there saying 'Uhm, Uhm, Uhm,' or maybe I would faint in front of everyone. Then when I told it and people laughed, it was so exciting. I wanted to do it again and again for an even bigger crowd. Now I know what it's like to be famous. If I hadn't tried, I would never have known how much fun it would be."

Storytelling involves taking a bit of a risk. But when you see the eyes of your listeners get bigger and bigger as you tell them a scary story or hear their chuckles when you come to a funny part, you will want to tell your story again and again. We've written this book because we know how much fun it is to tell stories, and we want others to discover the power and joy of storytelling as well.

If you haven't already, give storytelling a try. One of the hardest parts of telling stories is finding a good story to tell. We've made that easy for you by including 30 good stories to tell in this book, along with tips on how to tell them. So take these stories and tell them, whether to one friend while sitting on your front porch or to all the kids in your class at school. You can try them out at sleep overs or camp outs, while baby-sitting, and for family gatherings, especially during holiday time. Take a chance. Get off the couch, turn off the television, and delight your friends and family with a story.

Choosing a Story to Tell

Be sure the story you choose is one you *really* love. Maybe it makes you laugh or think a lot, or gives you a little shiver down your spine. If it's a good one for you to tell, you'll feel like you just can't wait to share it with someone. If you like a story, read it over at least five times before you make a decision on whether to learn it. If you *still* love it after five readings, it's a good one for you.

The stories included in this book are all excellent for telling. They are arranged in four sections, beginning with short "starter" stories and increasing in difficulty. There are some you will want to tell to your friends and others you might share with a younger brother or sister, younger classes at your school, or when you're baby-sitting.

Learning Your Story

The question that we are most often asked about learning a story is: "Do I have to memorize a story word-for-word?" Absolutely not! Most of the stories in this book are folktales, old stories that have been passed down through the ages. Before the invention of radio, television, videocassette recorders, and computers, storytelling was one of the main ways people had fun. Most stories weren't written down back then. People heard others tell them and then passed them along—and they always changed in the telling. The same thing happens if someone tells you a story at school, and then you retell it at the dinner table. You remember the basic plot, but you tell it in your own words.

Nowadays many folktales have been collected and written down in books. But just because the story you plan to learn is written on a piece of paper doesn't mean that's the only way to tell it. Pretend that someone has just told you the story as it is written down and set out to make it your own. Don't change what happens in the story. The basic plot should still stay the same. However, there are many ways to get from the beginning to the end.

Here are five ways to say basically the same thing. How many more can you think of?

> *Jack hurried down the road so quickly that he was soon out of sight.*

> *Jack tore down the road like a streak of lightning.*

> *You had to look twice as Jack sped by because he was moving so fast.*

> *Jack was running so fast down the road that he looked like a blur.*

> *Jack took off down the road so fast that he stirred up a cloud of dust that could be seen for miles.*

There may be a word or a phrase in a story that you're not comfortable with or have a hard time pronouncing. Ask an adult to help you with pronunciation. If you don't know what a word means, look it up in the dictionary. You may certainly substitute another word but be careful not to change anything that would alter the meaning of the story.

Some of the stories we've selected are not folktales but are by a particular author. An example would be "The Paper Bag Princess" by Robert Munsch. In this case it is important that you stay fairly close to his words since it is Munsch's own story. However, we're sure that even the author wouldn't tell the story using the *exact* same words every time.

Ways of Learning a Story

Storytellers have many different ways of learning stories. You will need to find what works best for you and for the type of story you've chosen. Pick one or two of the following methods; you certainly don't need to do them all.

Make a Written Outline

Use an index card to write the order of what happens in your story. Use *one* card so that you have enough room to write *only* the most important events. Here is the outline Daniel did for "The Mirror That Caused Trouble," a story found in this book on page 113.

The Mirror That Caused Trouble   Daniel Miller

1. Kim buys mirror in Seoul. He has never seen one.
2. Kim's wife finds mirror and cries. She thinks Kim has brought picture of a beautiful young woman.
3. Kim's mother says it's old woman.
4. Kim's father finds them arguing, looks in mirror and says it's old man.
5. Later, Kim and Chol's son finds mirror. He thinks boy in mirror has stolen his paper dragon.
6. Kim comes in and finds son crying.
7. Kim yells at man in mirror for stealing son's dragon.
8. Kim hits man and smashes mirror.

Draw a Storyboard

A storyboard is almost like a simple cartoon of your story. Don't think of it as a work of art but as a way of remembering your story. Use stick figures to draw the events in your story, one after the other, in the order events happen. Emmie did the storyboard shown below for "The Mirror That Caused Trouble."

When drawing your storyboard, use pencil so that you can easily make changes. If you want to include some dialogue in your storyboard, make a bubble coming out of the character's mouth and write what he or she says inside the bubble just like a cartoon. Use a key word or two rather than writing everything. For example, in "The Mirror That Caused Trouble" storyboard in Figure 2, the words "young woman" and "old woman" are used to show that the two women are arguing about what they see in the mirror. It's not necessary to write that Cho actually says, "Kim has brought home a beautiful young woman from Seoul to take my place," and then her mother-in-law replies, "Cho, there must be something wrong with your eyes! This is no young woman. She's old and not very good looking."

If one of the characters in your story is an animal you can't draw or that would take a lot of time to draw, do what Emmie did for the dragon in her storyboard for "The Mirror That Caused Trouble." She just wrote a "D" and put a circle around it. When you are done, someone may look at your storyboard and say, "What on earth is that?"

It doesn't matter if someone else understands your drawing, as long as you do.

Once you've finished your storyboard, try telling the story by just looking at your pictures. This will help you make the story more your own. Once you've told the story with your storyboard, go back and look at the written story to make sure that you haven't forgotten anything important.

Draw a Story Web

It may be easier for you to try and remember your story in "web" form. You begin with a bubble with the basic problem of the story and take it from there. Here is the web Leah did for "The Mirror That Caused Trouble."

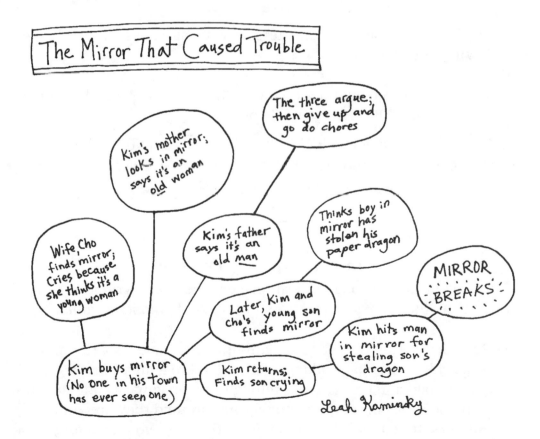

Make a Tape Recording

Many tellers find it useful to read their stories into a tape recorder and then listen to the tape over and over again.

Develop Your Characters

One of the best parts of storytelling is that you get to pretend you are all sorts of different characters. One kid wrote, "I like storytelling because it's a chance to act like someone you're not. I got to be a wizard, a fairy, *and* a magic chicken!"

Thinking about your characters will help you do a better job of acting like them. If there is a big bully in your story you may hold your shoulders high and speak in a loud, mean voice. It does *not* mean you should add a lot of details. For example, you wouldn't say how old the bully is or what he's wearing unless it was an important part of the story.

To help develop the characters in your story, ask yourself the following questions:

1. What kind of personalities do the characters have? Are they mean? Kind? Greedy? Brave? Angry? Foolish?

2. How do the characters look? What do they sound like when they speak?

3. How old are they? What do they look like when they walk or run?

4. How are the characters different from one another?

Practice, Practice, Practice

If you want to be a good baseball player, musician, writer, *or* story-teller, you must *practice!* Here are some ways of practicing your story:

1. Go over the story in your head anytime you have a spare minute— while riding the bus, walking to school, taking out the garbage, or lying in bed at night. Practice telling to an imaginary audience. If it helps, set up a few stuffed animals and pretend they are your listeners. If you find there is a part of the story you keep forgetting, practice that part a little harder and you'll know it the next day.

2. Practice with a mirror. This will help you think of movements or gestures. Make sure you are putting good expression on your face.

If possible, have someone videotape you, and then watch yourself to see what improvements you might make.

3. Practice with a friend or a parent. Stand up and pretend there are other listeners as well. Telling your story to listeners will show you the places where you'll want to work to improve your telling. Ask them to point out nervous movements that distract them from the story.

Telling Your Story

The story you've chosen is just words on a page. Your job as a storyteller is to bring words to life. You have many tools to work with—your voice, your face, and your body.

Change Your Voice

When telling a story it's very important *not* to speak in a monotone. This is when a teller says everything exactly the same way. After a while the teller begins to sound a bit like a robot and the audience will quickly lose interest.

Here are some of the many ways to change your voice that will make your story much more fun for you and your listeners.

Use Expression

Expression is the feeling or tone of your voice. It's a big part of what makes a story interesting. If a character is angry or greedy or scared in a story, the teller must convince the listeners that the character really feels that way. It wouldn't be much fun to listen to someone tell the classic story of "The Three Little Pigs" without making the wolf sound big and mean when he says, "I'll huff and I'll puff and I'll blow your house down!"

You can take the same word and say it with different expressions, and it will change the meaning. Take your name, for example. If you're outside and someone in your family calls your name, you can tell by the way they say it whether or not you're in trouble. If they call you in a nice, regular way it probably means something like, "Come on in, it's time for dinner." But if they yell your name, they're probably about to say, *"Why didn't you clean up this mess before you went outside like I told you to do?"*

If you have a dog, try this experiment. While looking right at the dog, say with an angry expression, *"You cute little dog!"* Despite the words you're using, the dog will think you're mad at it. Then say, using a nice and sweet expression, "You miserable fleabag." Even though you're insulting him, your dog will probably be wagging his tail and licking your face. Dogs don't understand meaning, but they do understand expression.

Change Your Volume

The "volume" of your voice is how loudly or softly you speak. You must be sure to always speak loudly and clearly enough so that all of your listeners can hear you. Look toward the listeners in the back often to make sure they are able to hear.

There are times that you will want to vary your volume. If a character is angry or excited, you would naturally want to make your voice louder. In another part of the story you might have a character who is scared, and it would be appropriate to make your voice quieter. If you have their attention, your listeners will lean a bit forward and listen a bit harder during a scary part. Varying the volume of your voice from normal to loud to soft is one way of creating different moods, and it will make your story more interesting.

Vary Your Tempo/Speed

Be sure to take your time when telling your story. If you rush, your listeners will have a difficult time understanding you. On the other hand, if you tell the whole story at a snail's pace you'll have restless listeners. The idea is to change your speed at the appropriate time in your story. Slowing down can suggest sadness, suspense, fear, or doubt. For instance, if you decide to tell the story called "Tilly" on page 47, you'll want to create an eerie feeling. Speak very slowly when the voice says, "Tilly, I'm coming to get you!" If you use good expression as well, you can make your listeners feel as if the strange voice is speaking right to them.

Speeding up at a certain part of the story can suggest excitement, nervousness, or joy. For example, you would want to say, "Jack tore down the road like a streak of lightning," very quickly.

Use Pauses or Silence

Sometimes in a story it is effective to actually stop and allow a couple of seconds of silence. This will help awaken the imaginations of your listeners and make them wonder what is about to happen next. For example, in the story "On a Dark and Stormy Night" on page 85, the main character hears a scratching noise at the window and pulls up the shade in his bedroom. When the teller pretends to pull up the shade, it is best to pause and look in horror to show the character's reaction to what he sees. This keeps the listeners in suspense a couple of seconds until the teller finally says, "There stood a creepy old woman …"

Change Your Pitch

Changing the pitch of your voice, how high or low you speak, is an easy way to show the difference between characters. Just for practice, try saying "Someone's been sleeping in my bed," the way Papa Bear, Mama Bear, and Baby Bear would each say it in the story "Goldilocks and the Three Bears." Another example would be the fable "The Lion and the Mouse." Try your lowest, meanest lion voice when the lion picks up the mouse and says, "I'M GONNA EAT YOU UP!" Then use a high, scared voice when the mouse replies, "Please don't eat me."

Whether you realize it or not, you change your pitch all the time when you speak in a regular conversation. Listen to one of your friends telling you about something exciting or scary that happened. As your friend tells the story he or she will speak a little faster and the pitch will get higher.

Use Character Voices When Necessary

Some stories like "Goldilocks" wouldn't be as much fun to hear without the contrast between the voices of Papa Bear and Baby Bear. And a story like "The Three Little Pigs" needs a mean wolf voice to make the story convincing. If you do decide to have a certain voice for a character, the character must keep the same voice throughout the story. If you start off with a great wolf voice and then forget to use the same voice later, the audience will be disappointed.

In most stories, it's difficult and usually not necessary to use a different voice for all the characters. You can show the difference between characters just by the expression in your voice and the way you hold your body.

For example, in the story "Who Will Close the Door?" on page 122, a husband and wife are very mad at each other. You don't need to have a low voice for the man and a higher voice for the woman. Instead, show the difference between them by holding your hands on your hips when speaking as the wife and folding your arms across your chest for the husband.

Emphasize Certain Words

When you put the emphasis, or stress, on a certain word it means that you say it a little louder and with more feeling than the other words in a sentence. It may even change the meaning if you change the word(s) you emphasize. For example, take the sentence "Did Martha give Mitch a red car?" and say it emphasizing the word in **bold** print below, and you'll have seven slightly different meanings:

Did Martha give Mitch a red car?   (You said she did, but did she really?)

Did **Martha** give Mitch a red car?   (Are you sure it was Martha? I thought someone else gave it to him.)

Did Martha **give** Mitch a red car?   (No, I think she lent it or sold it to him, not gave it.)

Did Martha give **Mitch** a red car?   (No, I heard she gave it to someone other than Mitch.)

Did Martha give Mitch **a** red car?   (She didn't just give him "a" red car; it was at least two or three.)

Did Martha give Mitch a **red** car?   (No, I saw Mitch going down the road in a brand-new blue car yesterday.)

Did Martha give Mitch a red **car**?   (No, I thought she only gave him a motorcycle.)

Use Facial Expression

The expression that you put on your face is an important part of storytelling. If you are telling about walking through the graveyard at night, you need to have an expression of fright on your face, *not* a smile. Practice telling your story while looking into a mirror and be sure the feeling in the story is shown on your face. Watching yourself on videotape can also be helpful.

Use Gestures to Help Listeners See Pictures in Their Minds

A gesture is a movement of your body that expresses or emphasizes an idea. For instance, you are making a gesture if you point toward the door as you tell your brother, "Get out of my room!" Gestures and movements, when they are done well, can greatly add to the effectiveness of storytelling.

Here are a few guidelines to help you use movements well:

1. Any gesture you make should help the listeners see pictures in their minds, *not* just you telling a story. If you do silly things that have nothing to do with the story, the listeners may laugh, but they will begin to lose the idea of the story. They will see *you* instead of the pictures in their minds. While telling "The Tortoise and the Hare," one child ran around the room like a whirlwind when the hare began the race. The listeners laughed, but afterwards they said they hadn't imagined a race but had only seen the storyteller. It would have been more effective if the teller had stayed in one place and put good expression in her voice, face, and body.

2. Concentrate on the expression in your voice and on your face. Many of your body movements will come naturally if you're using lots of good expression. For instance, if you sound very angry there's a good chance that your body is going to look threatening. If you talk like a big braggart, you'll find that you are holding your shoulders a bit higher. Remember, there isn't just *one* way to tell a story. Some people will use many more gestures than others.

3. Storytelling isn't the same as acting. Don't act out *everything* that happens; you are mostly *telling,* and leaving a lot to the imaginations of your listeners. Save your movements for times that will really add to your story. For example, often when you say a verb or action word it is a good time to make a movement. Take the following sentence for example: "The man *jumped* up, *grabbed* the sack, and *hurried* down the road." It is very effective if you emphasize the three verbs—*jumped, grabbed,* and *hurried*—with your voice, and make an appropriate gesture at *exactly* the same time you say the action word.

4. Make most of your movements from your waist up. This will allow your audience to see them clearly. For example, instead of showing that a character is running with your feet, use your arms and show how your upper body looks when you're running.

5. Avoid nervous movements. If a teller tugs at his or her shirt sleeve or rocks back and forth, it's hard for the listeners to concentrate on the story. Practicing your story over and over will make you feel more confident so you won't be as likely to make nervous movements. You probably won't even realize you're making them, so have a friend or parent watch your telling or have someone videotape you. If you move your feet a lot, pretend they're stuck in cement. If your hands are your problem, try putting them behind your back. Better yet, concentrate on keeping them still at your side, except, of course, when you wish to make a meaningful gesture.

Look at the Audience

If you've ever been in a play, you may have been told to ignore the audience or to look just above their heads. But in storytelling, it's very important to look right at your listeners. Otherwise, they may feel you aren't really interested in talking to them. You are counting on your listeners to be very involved in the story, and having eye contact helps to make them feel like they're on an adventure with you. If you tell "The Three Little Pigs," when you say, "I'll huff and I'll puff and I'll blow your house down," you will want to look right at the audience. Make them feel like you're the wolf and they are one of the little pigs.

If you look out the window or up at the ceiling as you tell your story, it will be hard to keep your listeners' attention. They will soon be looking up at the ceiling wondering, "Is there a leak up there or something?" or out the window thinking, "There must be something really interesting going on outside." You must keep your focus on the listeners in order for them to keep their focus on the story.

However, you don't always look right at the listeners when telling a story. At times you may pretend to "see" an object or a person. You might, for example, have a very puzzled look on your face as you pretend to look at an imaginary object in the palm of your hand. Or if you say, "Look into the sky on a starry night, and you'll see a white band of light called the Milky Way," you'll want to point upward and pretend to see it. When a teller looks as if he or she really sees something, it's easier for the audience to imagine it.

How to Begin a Story

When you go up in front of a group to tell a story, take your time. Look confident even if you have butterflies inside, since this will give your listeners confidence in you. Before you say anything, plant your feet and look around at your listeners. Be sure you have everyone's attention. If there are people in the audience who don't know you, introduce yourself and then introduce the story. You might simply say, "Hello, my name is Sam, and I'm going to tell you the story 'Who Will Close the Door,' a folktale from India." If your story is a folktale, it's important to say what country the story comes from. Your listeners will learn about the people who live in a certain place by the kind of stories they tell. After you introduce the story be sure to pause before you actually start to tell it.

If your story is not a folktale but is by a particular author, you might say, "I'm going to tell you a story called 'The Paper Bag Princess' by Robert Munsch." You might want to add some of the information we have included in our introduction to the story. For example, you could say, "When Robert Munsch started making up stories and telling them at a school, the kids demanded a new story every day. 'The Paper Bag Princess' was story number two hundred nineteen!" Better yet, make up your own introduction. If you were telling the story "Tilly" to a group of younger kids, you could say something like, "I used to get really scared at night in bed. Sometimes I thought there was a slimy monster in my room or a ghost in my closet. Raise your hand if *you've* ever been scared at night in bed. My goodness, that's a lot of you! Well, put your hands down and let me tell you the story of Tilly who was *really* scared. You see, there was once a girl named Tilly who loved to scare herself ..."

You should also think about whether there is anything in your story you need to explain before you begin. Perhaps you will be telling your story for very young children, and there's a word in the story you think they might not understand. It may be better to explain what the word means in your introduction, or you might just explain it when it comes up in the story.

How to End a Story

When you tell a story in front of a group, it is your job as the storyteller to let your listeners know that the story is over. Avoid saying, "the end," which takes away from the magic of your story and the power of the ending. Instead, for most stories you will want to really slow down at the end, and then take a bow and say, "Thank you for listening." The audience will then clearly know that it is time to clap.

We have taken care with the stories included in this book to write endings that sound final. If you find stories in other books you would like to tell but think the ending is not strong enough, write your own ending. If appropriate, you could add something like, "And that was the end of that." Or you can always say "And that's the story of ... (title of your story)" if necessary.

There *are* stories where you might speed up at the end. For example, there are a couple of stories in this book ("The Golden Arm" and "Tilly") that are known as "jump" stories because the whole idea is to make the listeners jump at the end. Once you yell "You've got it!" or "I've got you!" step back and take a bow to let the listeners know the story is over.

When the listeners clap, accept the applause graciously. Don't run back to your seat when they start clapping. Smile and say, "Thank you," and then walk confidently back to your seat.

Tandem Storytelling

Perhaps you've heard of a tandem bicycle—a bicycle built for two. In the same way, tandem storytelling means telling with a partner. We have included four stories in this book that are written for two tellers. We tell most of our stories together, and it's a lot of fun. Before you decide to pick one of the tandem tales, however, remember that it's actually much harder than telling a story by yourself. It will require a good deal of extra practice. Most important, you must tell it with a person with whom you work well and who enjoys the story as much as you do.

What makes tandem storytelling interesting for the listeners is the talking back and forth between the two tellers. It's important that the story flow smoothly between you and your partner. This is called "timing." Unless it is part of the story, there shouldn't be long pauses between your part and your partner's. One thing that will help you with your timing is to look at your partner whenever he or she is speaking. This will help you concentrate and prepare you to say your lines. If you're looking around the room when your partner is speaking, you may become distracted and forget when it's your turn. Also, you may distract the listeners, who, instead of listening to your partner, will wonder what you're looking at. Every so often, while your partner is speaking, you might act out what is happening in the story, but usually your focus should be on your partner.

Quite often in a tandem story, you will play one character and your partner will play another. These two characters will frequently speak to one another. If you and your partner turn and face each other while speaking, the audience will feel left out. Your voices will go off to the side rather than out toward the audience. Also, most of the listeners won't be able to see your facial expressions. The solution is to alternate between looking at your partner and the listeners. Begin or end your part by looking at your partner. During a long part you might look at your partner at the beginning and the end, as well as in between. During the rest of the time, concentrate on looking at the listeners and pretend they are the other character. When you turn toward your partner, almost always keep your lower body and feet facing forward. Turn only your head and upper body.

You might find a story you would like to tell with a partner, but which we have not written up for tandem telling. If so, you must take the time to sit down together and carefully plan out who will say what. When you practice you will probably make changes as you find what sounds best.

Have Fun!

Remember that the most important part of storytelling is to have a good time. After you read these stories you may find yourself sitting on your front porch telling one to a friend, or to yourself at night in bed, or anytime you're bored. Maybe you'll take that next step and tell your story in front of a group.

If you practice until you feel the story is a part of you, you will feel confident and will want to tell more and more. You can also make up your own stories, or tell about things that have happened to you, or look up some of the other suggested stories in our bibliography, *More Stories You Can Tell* on page 145. Pick a story to tell and have fun!

Thirty Stories to Tell With Suggestions on How to Tell Them

How to Use Our Suggestions
for Telling Stories

We have included suggestions to help you tell these stories. The story appears to the left, and the suggestions to the right. Read the story all the way through before you look at the suggestions. That way you can begin to think of your own ideas for how you might want to tell the story.

Read our suggestions, but remember that there are many ways to tell a story. Everyone tells with a different style, so feel free to make the story your own. We've included these suggestions to give you ideas, not because we think this is the only way to tell a particular story.

When we mention a "gesture" we are referring to a movement with your body that will help your listeners "see" your story. If you have trouble figuring out what we mean by a particular movement, ask a friend or a parent or another adult. When there are no suggestions on the right side of the page, it doesn't necessarily mean you shouldn't do a movement. We have not included every small gesture that people naturally make when talking. Everyone tells a story differently. Also, some stories call for more movement than others. The blank spaces will give you a chance to figure it out on your own.

When a word appears in **bold** print, you may wish to emphasize it, meaning to give it more power than the other words. Say it a little louder and with more feeling. Remember that your whole story should be filled with good expression, not just the words in bold print. As you practice your story you may choose to emphasize different words. That's fine—these are just suggestions.

At the top of each story we have written a little introduction. This is information that might give you more insight into the story. Although the information is mostly for you, you may want to share it with the audience as part of your introduction if it's appropriate.

Starter Stories

The Beautiful Dream

A story of the Navajo
(pronounced NAH´ -vah -ho) tribe
by Byrd Baylor

This story was written down by Byrd Baylor as she heard it from a Navajo girl named Lana Semallie. It's one of many stories in Baylor's book *And It Is Still That Way: Legends Told by Arizona Indian Children*. The native tribes of Arizona don't tell their stories in summer. The old people say snakes don't like to hear them and sometimes they get angry and bite the storyteller. So don't tell this story during the hot part of the year when the snakes may be listening.

Coyote **always**
liked to plan something tricky,
so one day he went walking
with Porcupine
and Brother Skunk.
He was thinking as he walked
along.

Have a very sly, tricky look on your face as you say this.

As you say "He was thinking …," pull on your chin with one hand and look as if you're up to no good.

Ahead of them
a wagon was going
down the road.

Make a gesture with your hand as if to point to the imaginary wagon. Pretend to see it with your eyes at the same time.

They saw a piece of meat fall off.

Look very excited as you point with your finger toward where the meat fell off.

They all **ran** for it,
and they all got there
about the same time.

Say "ran" very quickly. At the same time make a fast gesture with one hand starting from in front of your chest and moving out toward the audience.

But Coyote did **not**
want to share the meat
so he said,
"That's not fair."

Say this with a whiny voice. Put your hands on your hips and stomp your feet.

He suggested
they all race down a hill
and the winner
would eat the meat by **himself.**
So that is what they did.

The race started.
Porcupine curled up

As you say "curled up," lower your head a bit and scrunch your shoulders together.

and **rolled** down the hill.
He won.

As you say "rolled," make a rolling motion with your hands.

"That's not fair," Coyote said.

Again, say this with a whiny voice. Put your hands on your hips and stomp your feet.

Coyote suggested **another** plan.
He said, "The one who dreams
the most **beautiful** dream
will eat that meat."
So **that** is what they planned.

Coyote and Skunk went to sleep
but Porcupine stayed awake.
(pause)

Pause after saying "stayed awake" to build up the suspense a bit.

He had a plan of his own.

Sound and look very tricky as you say this.

26

Finally Coyote and Skunk
woke up and told their dreams.
They were both **good** dreams.
They were both **beautiful**
dreams.
Then they asked Porcupine what
he had dreamed.

Porcupine said,
"I dreamed I ate the meat."

As you say "I dreamed I ate the meat,"
you can rub your stomach and look like
you've just had a great meal, OR you
can make Porcupine lower his shoulders
as if he feels a little guilty.

They all **jumped up**
and looked in the tree
where they had left the meat.

Say this quickly as you look above the
heads of the audience at an imaginary
tree.

The meat was **gone**

Say this with anger and put your hands
on your hips as you say "gone."

and Porcupine was looking **fat.**

As you say "fat," make a gesture with
both hands to show an imaginary huge
stomach. Then take a bow to let
everyone know the story is over.

The Mysterious Box

*A story from Scandinavia
retold by Martha Hamilton & Mitch Weiss
Beauty and the Beast Storytellers*

If you've never told a story, this would be a good one to begin with. It's short and easy to learn, and younger children will especially enjoy hearing it. It's fun to tell because it may fool the audience into thinking it's a "jump" story, meaning you're going to jump and scare them at some point, but it isn't. Your listeners won't be disappointed because they get to join in at the end of the story.

One day a girl
was walking along the road

(It could be a boy if you prefer, OR you could also tell this story as if it happened to you and say, "One day I was walking …")

when she found a box.

As you say "she found a box," point to an imaginary box and "see" it with your eyes.

She picked it up.
It was wooden
with a little gold lock.

Pretend to pick the box up and look at it as you say this.

"I'll bet there's something **great** in this box! Maybe a treasure!"

Continue to hold the box, but be sure to look at the audience as if you're showing it to them. Sound very excited as you say this.

She **shook** the box and **heard a noise.**	Pretend to shake the box as you hold it with both hands. Look and sound excited as you say "heard a noise."
Then she tried to open the lid. She **yanked** on the lock. She **pulled** on the latch.	Pretend to hold the box with one hand while you act out the movements with the other. As you say "yanked," pretend to yank on the lock. As you say "pulled," pretend to pull the latch.
But that box would **not** open.	Sound frustrated and disappointed as you say this.
Then she thought, "Well, maybe it's best that I can't open it. There might be something **really creepy** in it. Maybe a poisonous snake!" so she put it down.	Say "really creepy" very slowly and as if you are disgusted. As you say "Maybe a poisonous snake!" shake your body as if to show a chill going through you. Have a scared look on your face through this part.
She walked on down the road, and soon she found a little key. She thought, "What if **this** key would open **that** box?"	Look and sound very excited.
She ran back to where she had left the box. As she picked it up and held it in her hands she thought, **"Maybe it is a treasure after all!"** She put the key in the keyhole, turned it, and **SNAP!**	Pick up the box and look very excited. Pretend to put the key in the hole and turn it. Say "SNAP!" loudly and make a quick gesture with your hands at the same time.
THE BOX WAS OPEN! *(pause)*	Look and sound very excited! While you pause, pretend to see what's in the box and show great surprise on your face.

But can anyone guess
what was in it?
Raise your hand if you have an
idea.

(Call on a few people and hear their
guesses. Then answer them.)

No. Put your hands down.
You're **all** wrong.
It was a **cow's tail,**

As you say "It was a cow's tail," show the imaginary cow's tail to the audience. Hold it between your two hands and look very surprised.

and if the **cow's tail** had been longer,

As you say "If the cow's tail had been longer," stretch your arms to the side to show the tail growing longer.

this **story** would have been **longer,** too.

Say this last part slowly and then take a bow to let everyone know the story is over.

If by chance someone in your audience has heard the story and answers "a cow's tail," you can still say "no" to their guess. Then at the end change it to "a mouse's tail" or any animal's tail (or other short item) that comes to mind.

The Night the Moon Fell Into the Well

A story from Turkey
retold by Martha Hamilton & Mitch Weiss
Beauty and the Beast Storytellers

This story is one of hundreds told in Turkey about a character called the Hodja (pronounced HO´ -ja; his full name is Nasrudin Hodja). He is what is known as a "wise fool." This character is based on a man who actually lived more than 2,000 years ago.

One night the Hodja
went to his well to fill his water jug.
He saw the reflection
of the moon in it,
and thought,

As you say "He saw the reflection of the moon in it," pretend to look down into the well with a worried look.

"Oh no!
The moon has fallen into the well!
How will people **see** at night?
The stars aren't bright enough.
But, not to worry!
I'll think of **some** way
to get it **back** into the sky
where it **belongs.**"

Sound and look very upset.

Make a quick switch from being worried to showing great confidence as you say "But, not to worry!" Point to yourself as you say "I'll."

The Hodja **rushed**
to get his fishing pole.
Then he let down his line and
hook and began to fish for the
moon.

At last his hook got **stuck** on the side of the well, and he shouted,	As you say "stuck," pretend to tug at the imaginary fishing pole.
"I've got you now! Don't you worry, Moon, you'll soon be **back** in the sky."	Again, say this with great confidence.
Then he **pulled** and he **pulled** and he **PULLED** until finally	Say "pulled" with great strain in your voice. Pretend to give a tug on the pole each time you say it.
UP came the hook	Make an upward motion with both hands as you say "UP."
and **DOWN** went the Hodja.	Make a backward motion with your body as you say "DOWN."
He lay there on his back, holding his **sore** head and rubbing his bruises.	Say this with pain in your voice. Rub your head and then pretend to rub a bruise on your arm.
But just then he looked up and noticed *(pause)*	As you pause, pretend to look up into the sky with amazement. This keeps the audience in suspense a bit before you tell them what you see.
that the moon **was back up in the sky!**	Sound and look very pleased and excited.
He forgot about **all** of his aches and pains. **"What a relief!"**	Sound and look very relieved.
he called up to the moon. "It **wasn't easy,** but thank goodness	
I was able to put you **back** where you **belong!"**	Point toward the sky as you say "where you belong!"
The Hodja felt like a **hero.** He went to sleep that night	Hold your shoulders high to show how proud the Hodja feels.
feeling **sure** that **he** had **rescued the moon.**	Say the last three words very slowly. Then take a bow so that your listeners know the story is done.

The Bundle of Sticks

A fable of Aesop
retold by Martha Hamilton & Mitch Weiss
Beauty and the Beast Storytellers

This is one of more than 200 stories told by a Greek slave named Aesop (pronounced E´ -sop). Although he lived over 2,500 years ago, his stories survive to this day because they tell such basic and important truths.

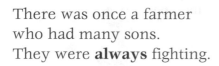

There was once a farmer
who had many sons.
They were **always** fighting.

Sound and look a bit disgusted as you say "always fighting."

So one day,
the farmer called his sons
together.

As you say "called his sons together," use both hands to make a gesture as if you are welcoming a group of people.

He handed each one
a bundle of sticks tied together
and said,

Pretend to pass out three or four bundles of sticks toward the audience.

"Sons, I want **each** of you
to try and break
this bundle of sticks in two."

Say this right to the audience as if you are the father and they are the sons.

Each son **tried** and **tried**
as **hard** as he could,

Each time you say "tried," pretend to try to break the bundle of sticks over your knee.

but each one failed.

Relax your body and sound a bit disappointed as you say "but each one failed."

Then the father
untied the bundle
and gave each son **one** stick.
He said,
"Now try and break
just this **one** stick."

Pretend to untie the bundle and hand three or four sticks toward the audience.

Hold up one finger as you say "one."

Each son **tried**
and each one
broke his stick **easily.**

Pretend to break the single stick across your knee easily as you say "each son tried." Then hold out both hands and have a look on your face to show that it was a cinch as you say "broke his stick easily."

"My sons," said the father,
"if you work together
you will be as **strong**
as that bundle of sticks.

Say this right to the audience as if you are the father speaking directly to the sons.

Gesture with both hands as if you are holding a bundle of sticks.

But if you argue,
you will be **weak** as that single
stick."

Hold up one finger as you say "single stick."

The moral of my story is:
Working together brings
strength.

Say the ending slowly and firmly, and then take a bow.

Who Will Fill the House?

*A story from Latvia and Lithuania
retold by Martha Hamilton & Mitch Weiss
Beauty and the Beast Storytellers*

**This is one of many stories from around the
world that tells of three brothers or sisters who
try to solve the same problem. In this story one of
the brothers comes up with a clever and unusual solution. The
story is told in Latvia (pronounced LAT´ -vee -ah [Lat rhymes with
bat]) and Lithuania (pronounced Lith -ooh -WAY´ -nee -ah [Lith
rhymes with myth, ooh rhymes with boo]), two countries that
border Russia.**

A farmer had three sons.
The two older boys always
bragged to the youngest brother
about how much **stronger**
they were.

As you say "bragged," hold your
shoulders high and have an expression
on your face that says "I think I'm the
greatest."

When the boys grew up,
their father built a brand new
house and said,
"Whoever can **fill** this house
will be the one to **own** it."

Point to and pretend to see an imaginary
house as you say this.

The **oldest** son
was sure **he** could fill it up.

As you say "he," point to yourself and
look and sound very confident.

He brought in a **horse,** a **cow, AND** a **pig,**

Either pretend to pull each of the animals into the house with a rope OR point to the imaginary cow, horse, and pig.

but they only took up **one corner** of the house.

Point to an imaginary corner and show on your face that you are not impressed.

The second son smiled to himself because he was sure that **he** would win the house.

Pretend to be very confident as you did for the first brother. As before, point to yourself as you say "he."

He brought in **bale** after **bale** after **bale** of hay,

Each time you say "bale," pretend to stack one bale of hay on top of another.

but they only filled **half** of the house.

Gesture with your hands to show half of the room, and show that you are still not impressed.

It was the **youngest** brother's turn. He brought in a small sack.

His brothers **laughed** and **laughed** when they saw it.

Point to the imaginary sack with a scornful look and a bit of a laugh.

He then took a candle out of the sack and lit it, and the **whole house** was filled with light.

Say "whole house" with amazement and make a big circular gesture with your hands.

So in the end it was the **youngest** son who got the house.

Say the last sentence slowly, and then take a bow.

Oh, That's Good!
No, That's Bad!

An American folktale
retold by Martha Hamilton & Mitch Weiss
Beauty and the Beast Storytellers

We have written this story in a form to be told by two tellers (A and B), although it can also be told by one person. If you do choose a partner, be sure it's one with whom you work very well. Telling with a partner requires a bit more practice, but this story is so much fun that it will be well worth the extra effort.

A: It was my friend Joe's birthday **just last** week.

Or Jane's—use any name you wish.

B: Oh, that's **good.**

Each time you say "Oh, that's good," be sure to sound happy and have a pleasant expression on your face.

A: Not **really.** You see, **everyone** forgot!

Shake your head as you say "Not really."

B: Oh, that's **bad.**

Each time you say "Oh, that's bad" sound very disappointed and as if you really feel sorry for your partner.

A: Not **SO** bad.
Because, you see,
we felt guilty and decided
to have a **big** party for him.

Sound optimistic each time you say "Not SO bad." As you say "SO," you might want to put both hands in front of you, palms up, to emphasize it even more.

B: Oh, that's **good.**

Remember to sound very excited each time you say this.

A: Not **really.** You see,
the party was going to be
in New York,
and Joe was in **California.**

Instead of saying "New York," you can say whatever city or state you live in. If you happen to live in California, then change it to another state.
When you say "New York," point to the right, and to the left as you say "California."

B: Oh, that's **bad.**

A: Not **SO** bad.
Luckily, another friend said
he would fly Joe to the party
in his airplane.

B: Oh, that's **good.**

A: Not **really.** You see,
when they were **halfway** there,
the plane ran out of gas.

Make this sound really terrible.

B: Oh, that's **bad.**

A: Not **SO** bad.
There **were** two parachutes
on the plane.

Put up two fingers as you say "two."

B: Oh, that's **good.**

Sound relieved.

A: Not **really.** You see,
Joe's parachute **didn't open!**

Have a feeling of despair on your face and in your voice.

B: Oh, that's **bad.**

A: Not **SO** bad.
Right below him
was a **huge** haystack.

When you say "huge," stretch out your arms to show how big the haystack is.

B: Oh, that's **good.**

A: Not **really.** You see,
sticking out of the haystack
was the **biggest** pitchfork
he'd ever seen.

Say this with great horror.

B: Oh, that's **bad.**

A: Not **SO** bad.
You see, when Joe landed
he **missed the pitchfork.**

Sound very pleased.

B: Oh, that's **good.**

A: Not **really.** You see,
he also **missed** the haystack.

Have a look on your face that says "Uh-oh."

B: Oh, that's **BAD.**

Use your best expression yet.

A: No, that's **good.**
Because that's the end of our
story.

Both A and B: Oh, that's **good.**

After the last line is spoken, both tellers bow and say "Thank you."

Next Step Stories

The Mouse and the Sausage

A story from France
retold by Martha Hamilton & Mitch Weiss
Beauty and the Beast Storytellers

Stories are often made up to explain serious things in nature. Others such as this one explain silly things. Let this story inspire you the next time you're trying to think of a topic to write about. Make up a silly topic such as, "Why Potatoes Have Eyes," "Why Lemons Make Your Lips Pucker," or "What Makes Popcorn Pop."

Once upon a time there lived
a **mouse** and a **sausage.**
And these two
were **SUCH good friends**
that they were **almost** like sisters,
so they decided
to set up house together.
They agreed to share **all** the work
that needed to be done.

As you say "mouse," gesture to the right with your right hand. Then gesture to the left with your left hand as you say "sausage." It's as if you are introducing them to the audience.

Every day one would stay home
and keep the house,
while the other would work
in their garden
or go to town
to buy anything they needed.

As you say "one would stay home ...," gesture to the right with your right hand. Then gesture to the left with your left hand as you say "while the other would ... "

One day the mouse
went to town
to do some errands,
and she came home
with a **hearty** appetite.
Oh, was she hungry!
And she found that the sausage
had prepared soup for dinner.
The mouse enjoyed the soup
SO much. She just went on
raving about how **delicious** it
was.

Pat your stomach to show how hungry the mouse was.

Sound very enthusiastic.

Finally the sausage said,
"Well, if you want to know the
secret, I'll tell you how I made
the soup taste so good.

Move a little closer to the audience and bend toward them as if you're letting them in on a secret.

I just **popped** myself into the pot
while it was cooking."

As you say "popped," you could either open your closed fist very quickly, or you could make a downward motion with one hand as if to show her jumping into the pot.

The next day it was
the mouse's turn to prepare
dinner. She was cooking a veg-
etable stew, and she thought to
herself:
"I'll do the **same** for my friend
as **she** did for **me.**"

Say this as if you're very pleased you can do the sausage a favor.

So she **popped** herself
into the **boiling** pot
(*pause*)

Say this part quickly. Use the same gesture as above for "popped."

without stopping to think
that a sausage can do **some**
things which even the **smartest**
mouse should **not** try.

Slow down and say this with a worried look on your face.

42

When the sausage came home,
the house was lonely and silent.

Say this line slowly.

She called out,
"Mouse, Mouse, where are you?"
(pause)

Look all around the audience as if you're looking for mouse. Sound worried. Then pause as if you're waiting for her reply.

but there was no answer.

Then she saw the cooking pot
on the stove
(pause)

As you say this, pretend to see the pot with your eyes.
As you pause, look down into the pot and have a look of horror on your face before you go on to say "and realized what …"

and realized
what her **poor** friend mouse had
done.

The sausage was **so sad.**
She just **couldn't** stop crying.
Even to this day,
when you hear a sausage
sizzling in the frying pan,
it's **really** the sound
of her **sighing** and **weeping**
for her friend mouse.

Sound very sad.

After you say the last line, take a bow to let everyone know the story is over.

How Coyote Was the Moon

A Native American tale from the Kalispel (pronounced Kahl -ih -SPELL ´) tribe of Idaho retold by Joseph Bruchac

Coyote is a trickster of many Native American tribes. Often his tricks don't work out as planned. If you like this story, look for the many wonderful collections of native stories retold by Joseph Bruchac.

A **long** time ago
there was **no** moon.
The people got tired
of going around at night
in the dark.
There had been a moon before,
but someone stole it.
So they gathered together
and talked about it.

"We **need** to have a moon," they said. "**Who** will be the moon?"

As you say "Who will be the moon?" gesture with both hands toward the audience as if they are all at the meeting and you are asking them.

"**I** will do it," said Yellow Fox.

Hold your shoulders high and point to yourself like a braggart as you say "I will do it."

44

They placed him in the sky.	Make a gesture with both hands to show how they placed him in the sky.
But he **shone SO brightly** that he made things **hot** at night.	As you say "shone SO brightly," squint and move your face and upper body backward as if a bright light had suddenly shone in your face.
Thus, they had to take him down.	Make a gesture as if to take him down.
Then the people went to Coyote. "Would **you** like to be the moon? Do you think **you** could do a better job?"	Look right at the audience as if you are asking them these questions.
"I sure would," Coyote said.	Once again, hold your shoulders high and point to yourself like a braggart as you say "I sure would."
Then he smiled. He knew that if **he** became the moon he could look down and see **everything** that was happening on Earth.	Smile a very sly, tricky smile as you say these two sentences. You may want to move your eyebrows up and down and rub your palms together to show Coyote's eager anticipation of being able to spy on everyone.
They placed Coyote up in the sky.	Again, make a gesture with both hands to show how they placed him in the sky.
He did **not** make the nights too hot and bright. For a time the people were pleased.	
"Coyote is doing a **good** job as the moon," they agreed.	Nod your head and look very pleased as you say this.
But Coyote, up there in the sky, could see **everything**	

that was happening on Earth.
He could see whenever
someone did something
they were not supposed to do
and he just **couldn't** keep quiet.

"Hey!" he would shout,
so loudly everyone on Earth
could hear him,
**"That man is stealing meat
from the drying racks."**
He would look down
over people's shoulders
as they played games
in the moonlight.
**"Hey! That person
there is cheating
at the moccasin game."**

Raise yourself up as you say this and look down toward the audience as if you're way up above. Point toward a part of the audience as if you're accusing them. (Don't point at one particular person or it may distract you or them.) Be sure to speak loudly during this whole part.

Point toward another section of the audience as if to accuse them.

Finally, all the people
who wished to do things in **secret**
got together.
"Take Coyote out of the sky,"
they said. "He is making **too much
noise** with all of his shouting."

Look angry and sound very upset as you say this.

So Coyote was taken
out of the sky.

Pretend to take Coyote out of the sky.

Someone else became the moon.

Coyote could no longer see
what everyone on Earth was doing,
but that hasn't stopped him
from **still** trying to snoop
into everyone else's business
ever since.

Say this end part slowly, especially the last two words.

Tilly

A story told in England, Canada,
and the United States
retold by Martha Hamilton & Mitch Weiss
Beauty and the Beast Storytellers

This is a classic "jump" story. Even if your audience knows what's going to happen, they will still enjoy the story. Take your time and build up the suspense. Throughout the story you should slowly move a bit closer to the audience so you can give them a good scare at the end.

There was once a girl named Tilly
who **loved** to scare herself.
She **bcggcd** her parents
to let her have her bedroom
in the attic because it was
the **scariest** room in the house.

Use a pleading voice as you say "begged."

One night, while in bed,
she heard a **strange** voice say,

"Tilly, I'm coming to get you!"

Each time the voice speaks, take a small step forward, and lean toward the audience as you say "Tilly, I'm coming to get you!" Speak very slowly and make the voice sound eerie and strange. You might want to move both arms with a wave motion to mimic how a ghost moves.

Chills went up
and down her spine,

Straighten your body and shake your arms out a bit. Have a scared look on your face.

but Tilly **loved** it.

Quickly change to a pleased expression.

47

The next night she heard:
**"Tilly,
I'm coming up the stairs!"**

Move and speak as before, except the voice should get a little louder each time.

Tilly was **excited.**
She had never had a **real, live, scary thing** happen to her.

Quickly change to a sound of excitement in your voice and on your face.

And the next night:
**Creeeaaak! Creeeaaak!
Creeeaaak! Creeeaaak!**

Each time you say "Creeeaaak!" have one of your hands climb an imaginary step in front of you. Alternate left and right. Have a worried look on your face.

and then,
"Tilly, I'm on the top step!"

Move another step toward the audience and speak a bit louder.

Now Tilly was beginning
to get a **little** nervous.

Show the nervousness on your face and in your voice.

She told her parents about the
voice but they just laughed.
Her father said,
"**Anyone** who wants her bedroom
in the **attic** has to expect
to hear **some** noises now and
then."

The next night the creepy voice said,
"Tilly, I'm at your door!"

A little louder, a little closer.

Tilly hid under her covers, shaking.

Hold both hands up beside your head as if you are holding the covers over your head. Look very scared.

The next day
Tilly asked her parents
if she could sleep in **their** room.
But her mother said,

"Don't be silly, Tilly.
It's just that **wild**
imagination of yours!"

Use a hand gesture to show the mother thinks this is ridiculous.

That night
Tilly heard the door open:
Creeeeaaaak!

Pretend to put your hand to a doorknob and open a door.

Then the voice said,
"Tilly, I'm in the room."

Louder and closer.

Tilly wanted to **SCREAM**
but nothing came out.

Look very worried as you say this.

Then it was closer.
"Tilly, I'm by your bed."

You should be right up near the listeners by now.

Tilly wanted to **run**
but she couldn't **move.**

Sound and look scared and desperate as you say this.

And then,
**"Tilly, Tilly,
I'VE GOT YOU!"**

Saying Tilly twice this time will keep listeners guessing about when you're going to jump. Say "I've got you!" VERY LOUDLY and make a jumping motion with your upper body at the same time.

*After you say, "I've got you," you
can end the story by stepping back
and taking a bow, **OR** you may
wish to add:*

Just then Tilly woke up.
But there was nothing there.

It had **all** been a dream.

Have a puzzled expression as you pretend to look around the room.

The Biggest Lie

A story from Russia
retold by Martha Hamilton & Mitch Weiss
Beauty and the Beast Storytellers

One definition of "storytelling" is "lying." Sometimes adults will say, "Don't tell me a story," when they really mean "Don't lie to me." Here's a story from Russia about a king who loved to listen to lies or "tall tales."

There once lived a king
who was **very** bored.
He had seen
all of the jester's tricks and heard
all of the storyteller's tales.
So he decided to hold a contest
as a way of amusing himself.
Messengers were sent to **every**
town where they shouted for **all**
to hear:

Sound very bored, especially when you say "very bored" and each time you say "all."

As you say "every," make a wide gesture with your hands.

"The king will give a golden apple to whoever can tell the biggest lie!"

Hold your hands up to the sides of your mouth like the old time criers used to do and SHOUT this!

Soon people began to arrive
from **all** the corners of the kingdom
to share their ridiculous stories.

There was the fisherman
who said he had just spent a **year**
living **underwater**
and the young woman
who claimed to have
ninety-five children!

You may want to think of other big lies instead of these to make the story your own.

When you are describing the lies, have a very doubtful look on your face.

The king enjoyed these tales
but didn't think there was one
that **stood out** from the others.

Then one day an **old** woman
carrying a **large** pot
appeared before the king.

As you say "a large pot," make a circle in front of you with both hands as if to show the pot.

He looked at her strangely
and asked,
"Do you need that pot to tell your
story?"

When you speak as the king, hold your shoulders high so as to look king-like and look slightly down as if you are peering from your throne. Always face the audience. Point to the imaginary pot and put a strange look on your face as you say this.

"Oh no, your Majesty," she replied.
"I need it to collect the pot full of
gold you owe me!"

When you speak as the old woman, put one hand on your hip and lean over a bit. Look up as if you are peering at the king on his throne. Use an old woman's voice if you feel comfortable doing so.

So that you won't continually have to say "the king said" or "the old woman answered," get your body into a position to show which person you are each time before you speak.

"A pot full of **gold!** Have you **lost
your mind?"**(king)

Say this with total disbelief.

"Oh no, sire.
Don't you **remember?**
I lent it to you just two months
ago." (old woman)

Speak with confidence each time you pretend to be the old woman.

"LIAR! I could sit here for the rest of my life and never hear a bigger lie!" *(king)*

Say this with great anger.

"If that's true, my Lord, then **you** owe **me** the golden apple."
(old woman)

Point to the imaginary king in front of you as you say "you" and to yourself as you say "me."

The king realized
that he had been tricked.
He had to either **give** the old
woman the golden apple
or **admit** that she had lent him
a pot full of gold.

Show with your voice and face that the king realizes he's in a difficult situation.

The king said,
"Well done!
You have won the contest
and the apple is yours."

Get your body ready to show that you are the king before you speak.

The old woman returned home
to her village with **not only** the
golden apple **but also** a great
story to tell.

The Biggest Donkey of All

A story told in Armenia
(pronounced Ar -MEAN´ -e -ah),
Turkey, and Russia
retold by Martha Hamilton & Mitch Weiss
Beauty and the Beast Storytellers

**There are many "noodlehead" stories told
around the world, probably because we all
like to laugh at someone more foolish than ourselves. The idea of
forgetting to count oneself is a theme common to many world tales
and is the theme of this story.**

One day a farmer told his son
to round up their **five** donkeys
to bring them to market to sell.
The boy tied
four of the donkeys together,
mounted the **fifth**

Use hand gestures to suggest tying the four donkeys together and mounting the other one.

and started on his way.

As you say "started on his way," move your shoulders up and down a bit to suggest the movement of riding on a donkey.

When he was about half way to
town he counted the donkeys
to make sure he hadn't lost any.
"One—two—three—**four?**
What?
Only four?
**Where could that fifth donkey
have gone?**"

Point to imaginary donkeys in front of you as you count. Count slowly and deliberately. Look and sound very confused when you say "four."

53

He decided to get off his donkey
and count again:
"One—two—three—four—**five!**
Oh good,
my lost donkey is back!"

Use a hand gesture to suggest getting off the donkey.

Again, pretend to count and this time act very surprised and pleased when you count the imaginary fifth donkey.

He was **puzzled**
(pause)
but **glad** to have
all his donkeys again.
So he **climbed** back on
and headed toward town.

Have a puzzled look on your face as you say "puzzled." Then switch to a relieved expression as you say "glad to have all his donkeys again."

Use a hand gesture to suggest getting back on the donkey.

The boy had not gone far
when he thought
he had better count **again:**
"One—two—three—**four?**
Only FOUR donkeys!
Now where did he go this time?"

Continue to count as before.
Again, look and sound very confused when you only count four.
Use the same gestures and voice expression as before.

He got down off the donkey
he was riding and counted again:
"One—two—three—four—**five!**
Oh good, he's back again!
I guess he hadn't
wandered **too** far away."

When you say "five" remember to sound very pleased.

The boy was **so** pleased
to have found his lost donkey
that he decided to **walk**
the rest of the way to the market.
It might take longer
but at **least**
he wouldn't lose a donkey **again.**

On his way he met a man who
asked, "Why are you **walking**
when you could be **riding**
one of your **donkeys?**"

Show with your expression that the man
thinks the boy is crazy.

"You won't **believe** this,"
replied the boy.
"Every time I **ride**
one of the donkeys I **lose** it.
But when I get down
I find him again!
Would you mind counting my
donkeys and telling me how
many there are?"

Say this with a baffled expression on
your face and in your voice.

The man began to count:
"One—two—three—four—five—
six."

Pretend to count in a very confident
way.

"SIX donkeys!" said the boy.
"That's impossible!
I left home with only five."

Sound and look very confused and
surprised.

Hold up one hand to show five fingers
as you say "five."

"That's **true,**" replied the man,
"but you forgot to count **yourself,**
for surely **YOU** are the
biggest donkey of ALL."

As you say "YOU," point toward the
audience as if you are pointing at the
boy. Don't point at one person and look
right at him or her. You may get
distracted or start to laugh if that person
responds. Instead, point to the middle of
the audience and look around at
everyone.

Why Crocodile Does Not Eat Hen

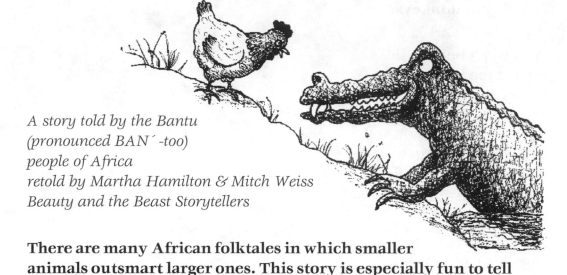

*A story told by the Bantu
(pronounced BAN´ -too)
people of Africa
retold by Martha Hamilton & Mitch Weiss
Beauty and the Beast Storytellers*

**There are many African folktales in which smaller
animals outsmart larger ones. This story is especially fun to tell
because there are lots of interesting movements you can make.**

Every day Hen went down
to the bank of the river
to hunt for food.
One day Crocodile
stuck his **big** head out of the water

As you say this, slowly raise your head
up as if you were lifting it out of the
water.

and opened his mouth **wide** to
eat Hen.

Put your two hands together and then
separate them slowly to show
Crocodile's big mouth opening. Be sure
to do this up and down, NOT side to
side, so it will look like a mouth opening
to the listeners. Have an excited look on
your face as if you're about to eat a
delicious meal.

But Hen cried,
"Brother, **please** don't eat me!"
She showed **no** fear of Crocodile.

Make a begging gesture with your
hands as you say this.

Crocodile was **so** surprised that

Have a look of confusion and surprise on
your face.

SNAP!
he closed his big jaws shut.
He was very confused.
He thought to himself,
"Why did Hen call me **brother?**
She is not one of **my** family.
I am a Crocodile and **she** is a Hen.
I shouldn't have let her fool me.

Tomorrow I will go **back** and eat her."

The next day Crocodile
stuck his **big** head out of the
water looking for Hen.
He saw her and said,

"Hen, today I'm going to swallow
you down in **one** gulp!"
and he opened his mouth **wide.**

"Brother, **please** don't eat me,"
Hen begged.

Once again
SNAP!
Crocodile closed his big mouth.
For some reason
he just **couldn't** bring himself
to eat Hen.

Afterward, he was **mad** at himself
again.
"Why did I let Hen go?
She cannot be a member of **my**
family. **She** lives on the **land.**
I live in the **water.**
I'm going to find her **right now**
and eat her up **once and for all!**"

Clap your two hands together as you say "SNAP!" to show Crocodile's mouth closing.

Look very confused as you say this.

Point to yourself as you say "I" and toward the audience as you say "she."

Begin to look angry.

Use the same motions as you did earlier.

Sound big and tough as you say this.

Use the same motions as you did earlier.

Use the same begging gesture.

Clap your two hands together.

Say this with great confusion on your face and in your voice to show that Crocodile just can't figure it out.

Say this with anger.

Gesture to the right with your hand as you say "land" and to the left as you say "water."

Crocodile got out of the river
and began to walk through the
woods looking for Hen.
Soon he met his friend Lizard
who asked,
"Crocodile, what's bothering you?   Say this with concern in your voice.

"Listen, Lizard, I have a problem.   Say this as if you're very annoyed.
Every day a **fat** little hen
comes down to the riverbank for
food. She looks **sooo** delicious
that my mouth starts to water
but just when I open my mouth
to **gobble** her up, she says
'Brother, don't eat me!'
Why do you think she keeps   Sound very frustrated as you ask this
calling **me 'Brother'?**"   question.

"Oh, that's **easy,**" said Lizard.   Say this slowly, pausing after each
"Ducks lay eggs.   sentence. Make a gesture with your
Turtles lay eggs.   right hand as you say "ducks" and with
I lay eggs, you lay eggs.   your left as you say "turtles."
Hen lays eggs.   Point to yourself as you say "I" and
    toward the audience as you say "you."

So in this way   Gesture toward the audience with both
we are **all** brothers and sisters."   hands as you say "we are all brothers
    and sisters."

"What a shame!
That good-to-eat Hen
is my sister,"   Sound very disappointed as you say this.
thought Crocodile.

So to **this** day, even though
Hen looks **very** delicious
when she comes down   Don't rush the ending.
to the riverbank,
Crocodile does **not** eat her.

The Brave but Foolish Bee

A fable of Aesop
retold by Martha Hamilton & Mitch Weiss
Beauty and the Beast Storytellers

Aesop (pronounced E´ -sop) was a slave who lived long ago in Greece. According to legend his master was so impressed by Aesop's wit that he freed him. This story is one of more than 200 stories that are referred to as Aesop's Fables.

One day while Lion was resting,
Bee **stung** him on the nose.

Say "stung" very quickly, and at the exact same time make a quick grabbing movement (bring your thumb together with your other fingers) toward the audience.

"Go away!" growled Lion.

Make Lion's voice deeper than your regular voice. Hold your shoulders high to show how big and strong he thinks he is.

But Bee replied,
"I'm not afraid of **you."**

Point to yourself as you say "I'm" and then toward the audience as you say "you." Make Bee sound very confident.

Lion **roared,**
"Don't you know that
I am king of the beasts?"
I could kill
a hundred bees
with one blow!"

Move toward the audience a tiny bit to make this part seem more threatening. Point to yourself the first time you say "I."

Hold up your fist as you say "with one blow."

"Let's fight and see," said Bee,
and he **stung** Lion by his eye.

When you say "stung," make the same
movement as you did earlier.

Lion tried to **strike** Bee
with his paw.

As you say "strike," make a gesture with
your open palm as if to swat a fly.

But Bee was **so** quick
that Lion hit his **own** face instead.

Point toward yourself with both hands
as you say "hit his own face instead."

Then Bee **stung** Lion
right on the nose.

Make the same hand gesture as you say
"stung." Point to your nose as you say
"right on the nose."

Again Lion tried to **strike** Bee
but only hit himself.

As you say "strike," make the same
gesture with your open palm as if to
swat a fly.

"I'll catch you yet!" boomed
Lion.

Sound and look very angry. Gesture
toward the audience like you're
threatening them.

But Bee wasn't scared.
He **stung** Lion on his lip.

Same movement as before.

Lion was **furious** by now.
He hit **harder** and **harder.**

Sound even more angry.
Make a karate chop type motion with
your hands each time you say "harder"
and "again."

Bee stung Lion **again** and **again.**
Each time Lion hit **himself** instead.

Point toward yourself as you say
"himself."

At last Lion's face was **so** bruised
he couldn't stand it **any** longer.

Say "so bruised" with great pain in your
voice.

He **ran away** as fast as he could.	Say "ran away" very quickly and at the same time make a fast hand movement starting from your body and going out toward the audience.
"NOW," bragged Bee, **"*I* am the king of the forest!"**	Say this with great confidence. Point to yourself as you say "I."
Bee landed on a bush to rest. But he didn't see the web which Spider had **just** finished spinning.	
"Oh no, I'm caught!" cried Bee.	Say this with fear to show the great trouble Bee is in.
He struggled to get free,	Say "struggled" with a lot of feeling and at the same time move your upper body to show the feeling of struggle.
but the web **grabbed** his wings	Make a grabbing motion with one hand as you say "grabbed."
and held him **fast.**	Keep your hand open after the grabbing motion and then close it firmly into a fist as you say "fast."
"I may have fought a **big** lion and won but I will **never** escape from this **little** spider."	Say this part sadly, with your shoulders a bit slumped to show that Bee sees there is no hope left for him.
And sure enough, the spider made a meal of him in **no** time, and **that** was the **end** of the **brave but foolish Bee.**	Snap your fingers as you say "no." Say the last part very slowly.

Fox and His Tail

A story from Mexico and Nicaragua
(pronounced Nik -a -ROG´-wah)
retold by Martha Hamilton & Mitch Weiss
Beauty and the Beast Storytellers

"Sly" and "clever" are often used to describe foxes. This is a story about a fox who is too clever for his own good.

Fox was walking along one day thinking how **brave** and **clever** he was.	Hold your shoulders high and sound very proud as you say this.
Suddenly some big dogs began to **chase** him.	Say this sentence very quickly. As you say "chase," make a fast hand movement from your chest going out toward the audience.
Fox ran as **fast** as he could,	Make a running motion with your arms and upper body.
with the dogs **close** at his heels.	As you say this, look back slightly as if to see the dogs and look very worried. If you turn your head too much, the audience may not be able to hear you.
Just ahead he saw a small cave,	Point to the cave in front of you and pretend to see it with your eyes.
and **dashed** into it.	As you say "dashed," make a fast hand movement toward the audience.

The big dogs
snarled and **barked** outside,
for the cave opening was **too**
small for them to fit through.

Say "snarled" and "barked" with a lot of meanness.

Fox **huffed** and **puffed**
until at **last** he got his breath.
Now that he was safely
in the cave,
he began to feel **very** brave
again.

Say this sentence as if you're out of breath.

He wanted to **brag**
about how **clever** he had been
to escape those dogs,
but there was no one
in the cave to talk to.

As you did at the beginning of the story, hold your shoulders high and sound very proud as you say this.

So he began to talk
to his body parts.
First, he spoke to his feet:
"Feet, what did **YOU** do
to help me get away
from those big dogs?"

Look down and gesture toward your feet as you say "feet," and then out toward the audience for the rest of the question. Point toward the audience as you say "you." Try to look at everyone, not just one person.

"We ran and **ran,**" said the feet.
"If we hadn't run so fast, those
big dogs might be eating **YOU**
right now!"

Point toward yourself with a proud look as you say "We ran and ran."

Point toward the audience as you say "YOU."

"That's true," said Fox.
"You are **good** feet."
Next Fox asked,
"Ears, what did **YOU** do
to help me get away from those
big dogs?"

Nod your head and sound pleased.

Gesture toward your ears as you say "ears" and then out toward the audience for the rest of the question. Point toward the audience as you say "YOU." Try to look at everyone, not just one person.

"We **listened.** Why, if we hadn't
heard those dogs coming from
behind, they would have caught
YOU for sure."

Again, point toward yourself with a proud look as you say this, and point to the listeners as you say "YOU."

"That's true," said Fox.
"You are **good** ears."

Nod your head as before. You might also pull on your chin with one hand at the same time.

"And now **you,**
Eyes, what did **YOU** do
to help me escape?"

Movements as before, except this time with the eyes.

"We **looked!** We saw this cave
and told you to go in it!
YOU might **still** be running if
not for **US.**"

Point to the listeners once more as you say "YOU" and to yourself as you say "US."

"That's true.
You are **good** eyes.
I'm such a **brave and clever Fox.**
I have such good feet,
ears, **and** eyes."

Show with your body and voice that Fox feels extremely proud of himself.

He reached over
to pat himself on the back,
and saw his tail.
"Tail, what about **you?**
What did **you** do to help me?
Why, you did **nothing.**
You just **sat there** while
those dogs **grabbed** at you!"

Reach to pat your back with your left hand and look over your right shoulder. Pretend to see your tail, but then turn and talk to the audience as you ask the questions with an angry voice.

Make a hand gesture as if to tell someone to "go away!" as you say "nothing," and then a grabbing motion as you say "grabbed."

Fox's words made
the tail **very** angry.
"You're right! I even **waved my
tail** to tell the dogs
to **come and get you!**"

Make the tail sound very angry.
As you say "waved my tail," wave one of your hands back and forth in front of you.

Now Fox was **furious.**
"That's true! You're a
BAD tail. I don't
want to see you **again!**"
And with that Fox
backed his tail out of the cave.

Have a feeling of extreme anger on your face and in your voice.

As you say "backed his tail," stick your backside out a bit and move back slightly.

The big dogs,
who were still waiting outside,
saw the tail and **pounced.**

As you say "pounced," make a grabbing motion with your hands.

And that was the end
of Fox and **his** tail.

Slow down for this sentence to let the listeners know you're nearing the end. Because they may think it ends here, hold your index finger up right after you say "tail" to let them know you have something else to say.

And **this** is the end of **my** tale.

Say the last line slowly, pointing to yourself as you say "my."

Bat Plays Ball

*A story told by the Creek tribe of the
southeastern United States
retold by Martha Hamilton & Mitch Weiss
Beauty and the Beast Storytellers*

**This is one of many stories from
around the world that explain
something curious in nature. Bats,
even though they have wings, are
not considered to be birds. In
every other way they are like
mammals. For example, they have fur, teeth, and a four-chambered
heart.**

> **The ball game referred to in this story was probably racket or
> stick ball, similar to the game of lacrosse.**

Long ago no one could figure out
whether bats were birds or animals.
The people of the Creek tribe
say that it was a ball game
which **finally** helped decide
what kind of creatures bats **really**
are.

As you say "birds," gesture with your
right hand, then with your left as you
say "animals."

One day the birds
challenged the animals
to a ball game.
Just when they were ready to
play,
Bat came along.
He wanted to play, **too.**

First he went to the animals' side
and asked,
"May I play on **your** team?"

Gesture with your hand toward the right
side of the audience as you say this.
When you ask "May I play on your
team?" put out both arms with palms
up and speak to the right side of the
audience as if they're the animal team.

The leader of the animals,
a **big** panther, said:
"**You** can't play on **our** team.
You have **wings.**"

Hold your shoulders high to show how
tough Panther thinks he is.
As you say this, make a hand gesture as
if to say "Go away!" Sound very
annoyed.

So Bat flew over to the birds and
asked,
"May I play on **your** team?"

Make a gesture with your left hand
toward the left side of the audience.
Then ask them the question as if they
are the birds' team.

But their leader, a **huge** crane,
said,
"**You** can't be on **our** team.
You have **fur** and **teeth**."

Show with your body that Crane is also
a bit of a bully. Make the same "Go
away!" gesture described above and
sound just as annoyed.

Poor Bat.

Say this very sadly.

Neither the animals **nor** the birds
would claim him as one of their
own.

Point to the right as you say "animals"
and to the left as you say "birds."

But Bat didn't give up.
He flew **back** to the animals.
"**Please,** let me be on your team.
I have **teeth** and **fur.**
I am an animal."

Say this with a lot of confidence.
As you say "teeth and fur," point to
your teeth and body.

The animals were not so sure
about this, but at last Panther said,
"**All right,** you can be on our
team.
But for now sit on the side
because you're too little to play."

Point toward the side.

Bat was happy
to at **least** be on the team.
He sat and watched
as the game began.

As you say this, look as if you're
excitedly watching a game.

It didn't take long
for Bat to realize
that the birds would win **easily.**
Every time the ball
went up into the air,
one of the birds

Say this with concern in your voice.

flew up and **caught** it.
Time and again the ball
went **much** too high for the
animals.

As you say "flew up," make a gesture
with one arm going up toward the sky.
When you say "caught it," make a
grabbing gesture with your hand as if
catching a ball.

Bat **begged** Panther to let him
play, but Panther said,
"**Sit down**
and stay out of the way
before you are **run over**
by the **bigger** animals!"

Say this with anger. As you say "Sit
down," make a very forceful gesture
with your finger pointing down.

The next time the ball flew
high up into the air,

Look up and pretend to see the ball
going into the air.

Bat couldn't stand it **any** longer.

Say this as if you're very impatient.

He flew after it **as fast** as he
could.

When Panther saw Bat
going after the ball,
he was about to **yell** at him
to sit down.

But when Bat **flew up**
and **caught** the ball

As before, when you say "flew up,"
make a gesture with one arm going up
toward the sky. When you say "caught,"
make a grabbing gesture with your hand
as if catching a ball.

just before Crane got it,
Panther was **so** impressed
that he let Bat stay in the game.

Say this with amazement.

For the **rest** of the afternoon
Bat was the **star**
of the animals' team.

He was **so small and so quick**
that he beat the birds to the ball.
Bat caught the ball
SO many times
that in the end
the animals won the game.

Sound very proud as you describe how
Bat helped win the game.

They crowded around Bat
and praised him.

"Good job!" said Panther.
"You may have wings,
but you also have **fur and teeth.**
You **must** be an animal."

Say this with a lot of enthusiasm.

And since that time
Bat has been counted
as one of the **animals.**

Do They Play Soccer in Heaven?

A story from American folklore
retold by Martha Hamilton & Mitch Weiss
Beauty and the Beast Storytellers

This story was inspired by "The Bad News" from Alvin Schwartz's *More Scary Stories to Tell in the Dark*. That story is about baseball and was told to Schwartz by a twelve-year-old girl. Take this story and make it your own. You could tell it about football or any other sport you like best. It could be about boys or girls.

We have written this story in a form to be told by two tellers (A and B), although it can also be told by one person. If you do choose a partner, be sure it's one with whom you work very well.

A: There were once two girls named Sue and Kate who were **very** good friends. They enjoyed eating, talking, and having adventures together.

Change to two boys if you'd prefer. Point to your partner as you say "Sue" and to yourself as you say "Kate."

You could say the things you enjoy most doing with your friends.

70

B: But **most of all**
they **loved** playing soccer together.   Say this as if they really enjoy it.
Sue was a fullback
and Kate the goalie.
They were teammates
on the town team   If you have a local town team, use its
and then in high school.   name here.

A: They even went to college   Use the real name of a nearby college if
together and played on the soc-   you'd like.
cer team. One day Kate said to
Sue,
"This is **so** much fun.
Do you think we'll **still** be playing soccer when we're older?"

B: "I certainly hope so."

A: Well, they **DID** get older
and they **DID** keep on
playing soccer.
They played with a group of
women **every** Sunday afternoon
just for fun **and** to keep in shape.

B: They both lived
to **quite** an old age.

They couldn't play soccer any-   Say this with disappointment.
more.

But they still **loved** to go   Change to a pleased expression as you
and watch their grandchildren   say this.
play on the local team.
One day Sue said to Kate,
"I wonder if they   Say this with a puzzled look on your
play soccer up in heaven."   face.

71

A: "Hmm, I don't know. That sure would be nice, wouldn't it?

As you say "Hmm," put your hand on your chin to show you're thinking.

B: "Let's make a pact.
Whoever dies first
will try and come back
to let the **other** one know
if they play soccer up there."

Point up as you say "up there."

A: "It's a deal."

Shake hands with your partner as you say this.

B: Time went by, and it turned out to be Sue who got to heaven first.

A: Kate couldn't **wait** for Sue to return.
Days and weeks passed,
and Kate had **just** about
given up hope.

Sound impatient.

But then one afternoon,
Sue appeared at her door!
Kate was **so excited**!
"**Sue!** Come on in!
Sit down and tell me
all about heaven.
But before anything else,
I've just **got** to know,
DO they play soccer up there?"

Change to a feeling of excitement at this point.

Look at your partner as you say "Sue!" Make a gesture as you say "Come on in!" Be sure to look at the audience part of the time as you speak to Sue.

Ask this with great curiosity, as if you just can't wait to find out.

B: "Well, Kate,
to answer your question,
I have some **good** news
AND some **bad** news.
Which do you want first?"

Don't rush this part.

When you say "good," sound hopeful. When you say "bad," sound a little nervous.

A: "Give me the good news."

Sound excited.

B: "The **good** news is that soccer is **very** popular up in heaven.
I play fullback,
and you won't believe this,
but I've gotten **faster** since I died."

Sound very happy as you say this.

Say this with disbelief.

A: "That's great, Sue.
But what's the **bad** news?"

Sound very pleased as you say "That's great, Sue." Then sound nervous as you ask "But what's the bad news?" Say it slowly as if you don't really want to know.

B: "The **bad** news is that I happened to look at the schedule
(pause)

Pause after "schedule" to build suspense.

and **YOU** are supposed to be goalie
(pause)

Point to your partner as you say "YOU."

tomorrow!
(pause)

Teller A should look shocked.

And who knows? Sue and Kate are probably **still**
playing soccer in
heaven!"

Both tellers should bow at the same time to let listeners know the story is over.

Challenging Stories

Bracelets

retold from a story
by Laurel Hodgden*

**This is a fun story to tell
because your listeners
get to join in with you.
It's a "modern" story
so it has a different feel
from many of the folk tales.**

Ellin's birthday was coming,
and her mother asked her,
"What do you want for your
birthday?"

"I'd like a bracelet," said Ellin.

"Okay," said her mother.
"What else do you want?"

"Can I have **another** bracelet?"

Show with your body the difference
between the mother and Ellin. When you
speak as the mother, hold your shoulders
up a bit higher and look at the audience
as if they are Ellin. When you speak as
Ellin, scrunch your shoulders down and
look up over the audience's heads as if
you're a child looking up at a tall adult.

"Yes, of course," said her mom,
"but is that **all** you want this year
—**just bracelets?**"

Say this as if you can't believe it's true. Hold your two hands out with palms up as you say "just bracelets?"

"Yup!" said Ellin.

Look very excited and nod your head as you say "Yup!"

Her birthday arrived.
Ellin opened the first package.
Inside was a **beautiful** bracelet.
She put it on.
She opened the second package;
inside was a **silver** bracelet.
She put it on.
She opened the third package,
and inside was a **gold** bracelet,
so she put it on, too.

Pretend to open each package, see the bracelet, and then put it on.

Be sure your face lights up each time you pretend to see the bracelet and when you say "She put it on."

Ellin looked at her mother and said,
"More."

Say "more" with a great deal of expression and with a very greedy look on your face. Put both hands in front of you, palms up, and move them as if you were begging. Then say to the audience "Why don't you do that with me? Let's try it." Then lead them so they can practice once before you go on with the story.

Ellin's mother,
being a good shopper,
went out and bought her
more bracelets,
enough to cover her
whole right arm!
Ellin looked at her mother and said,
"More."

As you say "whole right arm" use your left hand to point to your right arm from your shoulder to your fingers. Just before you say "More," motion for the audience to join in.

Her mother went out
and bought her plastic bracelets
—red, yellow, blue, green,
any color you could name.
They went **all** the way up her
left arm.

Use your right hand to point to your left arm from your shoulder to your fingers.

Ellin said, **"More."**

By now the audience should know to join in.

Ellin's mother put bracelets **all** the way up one of her legs!
"More."

Be sure not to rush or they won't be able to come in on time to do it with you. A good way to give them a cue is to get your hands in begging position and a greedy look on your face and pause just a second before you say "More!"

And then **all** the way up her other leg!
"More."

Act these movements out as you say them—putting the bracelets up each of her legs, and then up her body.

Ellin's mother put bracelets
up over her **body,**
up over her **neck,**
even up over her mouth!

Use both hands to show on your own body that the bracelets cover her neck. When you say "even up over her mouth," place your two hands just above your mouth and hold them there. That way you can make your voice sound a little muffled when you say "That's enough!"

Ellin said, "That's enough!"

But Ellin's mother
couldn't hear her,
so she put the bracelets
up and **up**
until they covered her **head.**

Gesture with your hands to show this.

Ellin stood there,
covered with bracelets.

Make a motion from the top of your body downward as you say this.

Just then
she felt a sneeze coming on.

Say this sentence slowly while looking very nervous.

"AHH, AHH, AHH, AHH, CHOOO!"

Speak in a medium quiet voice for the "AHHs." Have your hands in front of you and move them slightly as you say each "AHH."
Then say a loud "CHOOO!" and at the same time make a rapid movement with your upper body.

When Ellin sneezed,
she lost her balance.
She fell down and
broke **every single bracelet.**
Ellin got up,
dusted herself off,
and said,

Make a motion of falling with both hands as you say "She fell down."

Pretend to dust yourself off.

"MOTHER!"
"Next year for my birthday,
I'd like to have a necklace
**—JUST ONE,
PLEASE!"**

Remember to look up a bit as if you are Ellin looking up at her mother.

Show "one" with your finger as you say this.

Laurel Hodgden, a psychologist with the Headstart Program in Ithaca, New York, wrote this story in 1974 as part of a grant. In keeping with the oral tradition, Diane Wolkstein heard it from a student in her storytelling class, adapted it, and began to tell it. Carol Birch heard it from Diane, further adapted it, and wrote it down in Joining In: An Anthology of Audience Participation Stories and How to Tell Them. *Our version is adapted from Carol's.*

Skunnee Wundee
and the Stone Giant

An Algonkian
(pronounced Al -GON´-kee -en) Indian legend
retold by Richard & Judy Dockrey Young

The Algonkians include many Native American tribes who have similar languages. They live in the eastern and central United States, as well as in parts of Canada. Many of these tribes told, and still tell, stories of the Stone Giants. They said these creatures were enormous, made entirely of stone, and preyed upon the native peoples.

When people and animals
were **still** able to talk to one
another,
an Indian boy
named Skunnee Wundee
went out for a walk in the woods.

His mother had told him
never to go up the river
to the place
where the Stone Giants lived,
but the boy was **so** busy
skipping rocks across the river
he **forgot.**

As you say "never," point to the audience as if you are an adult warning a child.

Pretend to skip a rock.

Pretty soon, there he was, *(pause)* **right** in the middle of the circle of stones where the **Stone Giants** lived.	Do this part slowly. Look up and all around you as if you are in the middle of a huge circle of stones. Have a look of fear on your face.
He **turned** to run down river to the place where people lived,	With both hands in front of you, make a quick gesture with your body as if to turn. Don't actually turn—be sure the audience can always see the expression on your face.
but he ran **right** into the **feet** *(pause)* of a **Stone Giant.**	As you say "feet," pretend to see a pair of enormous feet right in front of you. During the pause, let your eyes go slowly from the feet of the imaginary giant up to his head.
The giant was as tall as a **pine tree.**	Look at the audience as you say "The giant was as tall as a" and then back up at the imaginary giant as you say "pine tree." Have a very scared look on your face.
The giant **picked** Skunnee Wundee up and said:	As you say "picked," pretend to pick the boy up and hold him in your open palm.
"YOU'RE A PEOPLE! I EAT PEOPLES!"	Pretend you are the giant looking at the boy in your palm. Use a deep, mean giant voice. Say this very slowly as if the giant is really having to think hard to figure this out.
"Oh, no," cried Skunnee Wundee, **"don't eat me!"**	Say this with a pleading voice.
The Stone Giant thought about it for a while.	Scratch your head and look as if you're really thinking hard.

Stone Giants are **not** very smart. **"WHY NOT?"** the giant asked at last.

Have a confused look on your face as you say "Why not?" Be sure to use the same giant voice as before.

"Because,"
said Skunnee Wundee,
"I can skip a rock farther across the river than **you** can."

As you say this, look up and pretend to see an enormous giant. Point to yourself as you say "I," and to the audience as you say "you," and sound very confident.

The giant had to think about that for quite a while.

Hold your chin with one hand and look very confused.

"I'll eat you ANYWAY."

As you say this, pretend to see the boy in the palm of your hand once again. Make the giant sound tough but not very smart.

"No, wait!" yelled Skunnee Wundee.
"Let me **prove** to you how well I can skip a rock."

Again, look up at the enormous giant.

The Stone Giant put the boy down
and picked up a boulder as **big** as an Indian family's **lodge.**
"I got my stone," said the giant.
"YOU pick yours."

Pretend to put the boy down and pick up an enormous boulder.

Point to yourself as you say "I," and to the audience as you say "you." Point at everyone, not one person.

Skunnee Wundee looked
all around the rocks
by the river,
trying to find a **good** flat one
to skip across the water.
He heard a little voice say,
"Choose **me**, Skunnee Wundee, choose **me**!"

Look around as you say this.

Use a higher pitched voice for the turtle.

There on the riverbank
was a **little** turtle,
just about the size
of a **good** flat rock.
Skunnee Wundee
picked up the turtle.
The turtle pulled its head and feet
into its shell
and tried to look as much
like a rock as possible.

But the stupid Stone Giant
was **very** easy to fool.
The giant **threw** his great big rock,
and it skipped **ten** times
along the water
before it sank into the deep river.
"Ten times," said the Stone Giant.
"I win."

"Not yet, you don't,"
said Skunnee Wundee,
and he **threw**
the little turtle into the river.
The turtle skipped
just like a flat rock,
two, three, four, **five** times.
Then the turtle put out its feet
and began to **kick.**
Six times the turtle skipped,
seven, eight, nine, ten.
Then the turtle began to **swim.**
Eleven, twelve, thirteen times,
the swimming turtle looked
like a skipping rock.
**Fourteen, fifteen,
SIXTEEN times!**
The turtle swam
all the way to the other side
and sat on the **other** riverbank
looking like a rock.

Point to the imaginary turtle on the riverbank, and pretend to see it with your eyes. Sound surprised and pleased.

Pretend to pick up the turtle.

As you say this, scrunch your head close to your shoulders and pull your arms close to your body.

Pretend to throw a rock as if you are trying to skip it across the water.

Hold your shoulders high when you speak as the giant. Make him sound like a real bully.

Sound very determined.

Again, pretend to throw a rock the way you do when you're skipping one.

Pretend to see the turtle skipping across the river. Pointing with your finger and making a gesture going toward the audience each time you count will help you to focus your eyes. You must really convince the listeners that you see it, and then they will picture it easily.

Your voice should sound a little more amazed with each number you count.

Sound very amazed and impressed as you count these last numbers.

Challenging Stories

"I win," said Skunnee Wundee.	Point to yourself and sound very excited.
The Stone Giant was **SO mad**	Sound angry.
that he **shook** and **shook** and **shook** himself	As you say this, hold your fists tight and shake your head and upper body.
into a **thousand** pieces. All the pieces fell into a **big** rock pile.	Make a big circle with both hands to show the huge rock pile.
Skunnee Wundee crossed the river, thanked the turtle, and went home. Don't ask how he crossed the river. That's a **different** story!	Take your time on these last two sentences.

On a Dark and Stormy Night

*A story from American folklore
retold by Martha Hamilton & Mitch Weiss
Beauty and the Beast Storytellers*

**In telling this story the
storyteller builds suspense in the
same way as for a "jump" story,
but it has a different kind of
surprise ending. Be sure to tell
it as if it is scary right up to the
very end. The best way to draw
the audience in is to tell the story as if it happened to you, so don't
introduce it by saying it is "retold from American folklore." If you
would feel more comfortable telling the story as if it happened to
someone else, you can change the main character to "my friend,
John" or "my sister."**

**The title we gave this story is a bit of a joke. It is a cliché, an
overused saying or expression, something good writers try to avoid.
Snoopy always begins his bad novels in the cartoon *Peanuts* with "It
was a dark and stormy night ..."**

Everyone knows **my** house.
It sits **all** by itself
on top of the biggest hill in town.

As you say "the biggest hill in town,"
gesture as if to show a hill in the
distance. Pretend to see the hill with
your eyes as well.

It's **always** windy up there,
so it's a great place to fly kites,
but it's **scary** when there's a big
storm.

Say "scary" with a creepy expression.
You may want to let a little chill run
through your body but don't overdo it.
You're just setting the mood.

84

One night I was in my room
sitting at my desk
doing my homework
when an **awful**
thunderstorm blew up.

Say this with spookiness in your voice.

Lightning **flashed,**
thunder **crashed,**
and the rain **pounded**
against the house.

Emphasize the word "flashed" not only with your voice, but also make a quick upward motion with your right hand. Make an upward movement with your left hand to emphasize "crashed," and then as you say "pounded" make a downward movement with both hands.

Suddenly,
at my window
I heard
"scratch, scratch, scratch."

Say "suddenly" quickly and have a very nervous look on your face.

Say this very slooowly. Look very worried. Hold both hands up toward the audience and make a scratching gesture each time you say "scratch."

I thought it was probably
just the branches of the old oak
tree scraping against my window,
so I went back to studying.

As you say "just the branches of the old oak tree," make a hand gesture as if to say "Oh, that's nothing."

The **"scratch, scratch, scratch"**
continued, and finally
I was **so** curious
I just **had** to know
what was making that sound.

Very slooooowly and make the scratching gestures again.

Say this as if you just can't help yourself.

I opened the shade,
and almost **fainted.**
(pause)

Open an imaginary shade. Put your hand on your heart with a bit of a gasp as you say "almost fainted."
As you pause, have a look of horror on your face as you pretend to see the old woman. This keeps the audience in suspense a bit. Then say "There stood a creepy ..." When you say "creepy," let a little shudder go through your body.

There stood a **creepy** old
woman,

the rain **pouring** down her face,
her clothes **dripping** wet.

Make a motion with your hands from the top of your head and down the sides as you say "the rain pouring down her face." Continue with the same motion from your shoulders down as you say "her clothes dripping wet." Keep a look of disgust on your face throughout this part.

But what **really** caught my eyes
were her lips and fingernails.
Both were painted
in the **brightest** shade of red
I've ever seen.

Say this with amazement.

Just then she said,
"I'll bet you want to know
what I do
with these **long, red fingernails
and red, red lips.**"

Lean over a bit like an old woman and speak directly to the audience. Keep a threatening look on your face. It also adds to the effect if you move your eyebrows up and down a bit. When you say "you," point toward the audience. Use the fingers of one hand to point to the imaginary "long red fingernails" on the other hand and then to your lips.

"No!" I screamed
and **pulled** down the shade.

Quickly pull down an imaginary shade as you say "pulled."

I didn't tell **anyone**
about the old woman
because I knew **no one**
would believe me.
After awhile
even *I* began to wonder
if I had **really seen** her,
or if it had been a dream.

Point to yourself as you say "I." Have a very puzzled look on your face and in your voice.

A few weeks later,
on another dark
and stormy night,
I was in bed reading a good book,
when I heard that same
"scratch, scratch, scratch."

Very slooowly and with motions, as before.

I didn't want to go to the window,
but it seemed as if
a **strange** force drew me there.

As you say "drew me there," put one hand out as if it is being slowly pulled toward the audience against your will.

When I pulled up the shade
there was the same
creepy old woman,
the rain **pouring** down her face,
her clothes **dripping** wet.
Again she looked right at me and
said,
"I'll bet you want to know
what I do
with these **long, red fingernails
and red, red lips.**"

Use the same motions and feeling as when the old woman appeared the first time.

Make the old woman have the same creepy voice she did the first time.

"No!" I shouted
and **pulled** down the shade.

The "No!" should be very loud.
Make a fast downward pulling motion.

But after that
I **couldn't** keep her **off** my mind.
Who was this **strange** old woman?
Why was she bothering **me?**
And what on earth **did** she do
with her long, red fingernails
and red, red lips?
I couldn't **eat.**
I couldn't **sleep.**

Keep both hands out in front of you, palms up, as if to ask "why?" as you ask all of these questions.

I was **always** daydreaming in
school.
I **had** to know.
So on the next dark and stormy
night,
I was ready for her.
As soon as I heard that awful
"scratch, scratch, scratch,"

I **rushed** over to the window
and **rolled up** the shade.

Sure enough,
there was the same old woman.
This time I **begged her:**
"What **do** you **do** with those
**long, red fingernails
and red, red lips?"**

And as I watched
the old woman **very slowly**
took one of her
long, red fingernails,

put it to her **red, red lips**
and went
(pause)

brmm-brmm-brmmm ...

Start to sound desperate, as if you think
you'll go crazy if you don't find out.

Very slooowly, and with motions.

Say this sentence very quickly.
Make a rapid hand movement to the
side as you say "rushed," and an upward
movement as you say "rolled up."

Focus your eyes to convince the
audience that you see the old woman in
front of you.

Say this with a pleading voice.

The audience is expecting to be scared,
so keep the feeling of suspense as long
as possible. Go very slowly. Hold up an
imaginary long red fingernail of one
hand as you say "took one of her long,
red fingernails."

Slowly place the tip of the fingernail at
the top of your lips.

After you pause, then quickly strum your
finger up and down over your lips a few
times to make the "brmm" sound.

Take one step back and take a bow to
let everyone know the story is definitely
over.

Clytie

*A Greek myth
retold by Martha Hamilton &
Mitch Weiss
Beauty and the Beast Storytellers*

**This kind of story is called a
pourquoi (pronounced pour
-KWA´) story. Pourquoi is the French
word for "why." Other pourquoi stories included in this book are:
"The Mouse and the Sausage," "Why Crocodile Does Not Eat Hen,"
"Bat Plays Ball," and "Why Anansi the Spider Has a Small Waist."
These stories attempt to explain something in the world.**

In ancient Greece
the god of the sun
was named Apollo.
Every day he drove his horses
in his sun chariot across the sky.
As he drove,
he shone **very** brightly
because he didn't want
anyone on the earth
to look up and see him.

Look up into the imaginary sky and
point with your hand to show the
chariot making its way across the sky.

At that time
there lived a girl named Clytie.
She was tall,
with **big** brown eyes and **golden** hair.

Clytie was **very** curious about
this bright light in the sky
that **no one** was supposed to look
at.

Sound curious as you say this.

One morning Clytie was
out in the garden near her house.
She saw that the sky
was full of clouds and thought,

Look up for a moment as if you were
looking up into the sky.

"If I were to look up at Apollo
today, the clouds would be like a
curtain so that he wouldn't see
me."

Sound and look a bit mischievous.

Clytie looked up and **there,**
between the clouds,
she caught a glimpse of **Apollo**
in his chariot.

As you say "there," point up to the
imaginary sky with a look of amazement
on your face as if you see Apollo.

It was such an **amazing** sight
that Clytie could **not** look away.

Look right at your listeners as you say
this.

Her eyes began
to follow his path,
and she **slowly** turned her head
to watch him
as he moved across the sky.

Look up again and let your eyes slowly
follow Apollo's path across the sky as
you say this.

After this Clytie spent her days
out in the garden
trying to catch **another** glimpse of
him. Clytie's parents warned her
that Apollo would grow **angry**
if he saw her staring up at him.
But Clytie **could not help herself.**
Now that she had **seen Apollo,**
she could think of **nothing** else.

As you say "grow angry," shake your
finger at the audience as if to scold
them.

Sound a bit desperate to show that
Clytie feels she absolutely must see
Apollo.

But **one** day
Apollo happened to **look down**
and **saw** Clytie staring up at him.
He was furious!
He drew rein on his horses

Pretend to look down from the sky. Look and sound furious as you "see" Clytie.

Pretend to draw rein on a horse—have an angry look on your face as you do this.

and looked **down** into Clytie's eyes.

Look down in anger as if you are Apollo and you see Clytie looking up at you.

Just then
a very strange thing
began to happen.

Say this sentence slowly and mysteriously.

Clytie's **big** brown eyes
grew **larger** and **larger,**

Describe the way Clytie changes with amazement. As you say "larger and larger," make a gesture with both hands to show something getting bigger and bigger.

until it seemed
as if she had one **huge** brown
eye which covered her **whole**
face.

As you say "one huge brown eye," make a large circle with your hands.

Her golden hair stood
straight out
in a circle around the eye.

Make a gesture with both hands to show Clytie's hair going straight out from her head.

Her body became a **tall** green
stalk.

Stand very tall and stiff as you say this.

And Clytie's toes changed into
roots which **sank** into the ground.

Point both of your hands downward to look like roots. As you say "sank," make a motion of the roots sinking into the ground.

When Clytie's mother
called her in for lunch,
(pause)

Have a worried look on your face as you say this.

there was no answer.

When she went outside
to look for her daughter,
all that she found
was a **tall, beautiful flower.**

> Pretend to see the imaginary sunflower in front of you, and say this with a hint of sadness in your voice.

Apollo had **changed Clytie**
into the **first** sunflower.

And **to this day**
if you notice a field of sunflowers,
you will see that
they stand **tall** and **stiff.**

> Stiffen your body and stand a bit taller as you say this.

But just as Clytie did long ago,
their **huge brown eyes**

> Make a large circle with your hands as you say "huge brown eyes."

turn to follow the path of the sun

> Look up toward the imaginary sun and move your head from left to right as your eyes follow the sun across the sky.

from morning until night.

> Say the last four words slowly.

The Golden Arm

*A story from England
retold by Martha Hamilton & Mitch Weiss
Beauty and the Beast Storytellers*

This is a classic "jump" story. The teller's main purpose is to build up tension throughout the story and then to startle the audience with a loud "YOU'VE GOT IT!" at the very end. If you create the right mood, this story can be told anywhere, but be sure to turn the lights down a bit before you begin. Our version is adapted from the story as written down by Joseph Jacobs, a famous English collector of stories.

Long ago in England
there lived a man
who traveled the land **all over**
in search of a wife.
He saw **young** and **old,**
rich and **poor,**
pretty and **plain,**
but couldn't find **one** to his liking.
At last he found a woman,
young, fair, **and rich!**

Gesture with your right hand as you say "young" and with your left as you say "old." Do the same with "rich and poor" and "pretty and plain."

Sound very excited as you say this.

What's more, her left arm
was made of **solid gold**
from her shoulder **all** the way
down to the tips of her fingers.
(pause)
He married her **at once.**

Point with your right hand toward your left shoulder, and then continue down your arm to the tips of your fingers.

Pause after saying "fingers," raise your eyebrows and look a bit greedy, and then say "He married her at once."

93

They settled in a small village
and lived quite happily,
but the woman often wondered
if her husband loved her
even **half** as much
as he loved her golden arm.

Say this with suspicion in your voice and on your face.

So every night she would say to
him, "If I die first
you must **promise**
to bury me **with** my golden arm."

While saying this look right at the listeners as if you are the wife and they are the husband.

And every night her husband would
reply, **"But of course, dear."**

Say this very innocently.

Sure enough the wife
did die before her husband.
He wore the **blackest black**
and put on the **saddest face**
at her funeral.

As you say "He wore the blackest black," use both hands to point from your shoulders and down your body as if to show the clothes you are wearing.

But that night he lay awake
thinking about the golden arm
and **all** the things
that he could buy with it.
Finally he got out of bed
and **trudged** up the hill
to the **dark graveyard.**
He dug up the body,
grabbed the golden arm
and hid it inside his coat.

Show greed on your face and in your voice as you say this.

Say "trudged" with strain in your voice.

Pretend to grab the arm and put it inside your coat.

On the way home
a **harsh** wind began to blow
and the man **shivered** and **shook**
because the golden arm
was as **cold as ice.**

Say this part with great feeling. As you say "shivered and shook," scrunch up your shoulders and let an imaginary chill go down your spine.

When he finally got home,
he **jumped** into bed
and crawled underneath the
covers trying to warm himself
up. He put the golden arm
underneath the pillow next to
him. At last he managed
to stop shaking
(*pause*)

Say this quickly.

After you say "shaking," heave a big
sigh of relief. As you pause, begin to get
a terrified look on your face and then
say "but then suddenly …"

but then **suddenly**

he heard a voice **way** off down
the road saying,
**"Where's my golden arm?
Who's got my golden arm?"**

Say this slowly, with suspense in your
voice.

Slowly, with anger in your voice; it
should also be said softly but loud
enough for everyone to hear you.

The man thought
he must be hearing things.
It was probably just the wind.

Say this quickly and show that the man
is trying to convince himself that it's
nothing.

But a few minutes later
there was that same voice
but this time it sounded
as if it were **right** at his front
door: **"Who's got my golden
arm?"**

Say this slowly and with more terror on
your face and in your voice.

Each time you say "Who's got my
golden arm?" move a little closer to the
audience and make your voice a bit
louder.

He wanted to jump out of bed
and run, but the **only** way out
was **down** the steps,
and he could hear **something**
coming up.

Speak quickly and sound desperate and
scared.

The stairs **creaked** and **groaned**
and the voice repeated, **"Who's
got my golden arm?"**

Do this part very slowly.
Move toward the audience.

Just then the bedroom door
opened.

CREAK!!!

As you make a creaky door noise,
pretend to open the door. Have a
terrified expression on your face as if
you are the man wondering what is
going to come through the door.

and in walked **the ghost**
of his dead wife,
her face **paler** than milk,
her eyes **staring** at nothing,
all the time **wailing:**
"Who's got my golden arm?"

Have a horrified look on your face as
you pretend to see the ghost.

You should be right up near the
audience looking them in the eyes by
now so that the ending will have the
maximum effect.

The ghost glided over to his bed,
looked him **right** in the eye and
said,
"Who's got my golden arm?"

Look all around the audience as you
continue to move up. You could say
"Who's got my golden arm?" twice this
time to keep listeners wondering when
you're going to jump.

"YOU'VE GOT IT!"

Use your whole body for this! Say it very
loudly and make a jumping motion with
your hands toward the audience. You
will startle them more if you say the final
"Who's got my golden arm?" and then
turn quickly to the other side as you
shout "You've got it!" Then step back,
take a bow and say "Thank you," so
that your listeners will know for sure
that you're done.

The Silversmith and the Rich Man

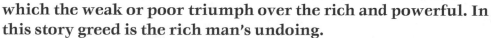

*A Jewish tale
retold by Martha Hamilton &
Mitch Weiss
Beauty and the Beast
Storytellers*

**Since folktales were
mostly created and told
by common people,
there are many stories in
which the weak or poor triumph over the rich and powerful. In
this story greed is the rich man's undoing.**

**A good deal of this story consists of dialogue between the two
characters. You may wish to turn your head and upper body
slightly to the left when speaking as the silversmith, then to the
right for the rich man. Don't turn too far or your voice will project
to the side rather than out toward the audience.**

In a village
there lived a **poor** silversmith.

Although he struggled
to make ends meet,
somehow he **always** managed
to get by because he was so clever.

This man had a **very** rich neighbor,
and one day the silversmith went to
the rich man's house and asked to
borrow a **large** silver spoon.

The rich man agreed but said, "You must **promise** to return it **tomorrow.**"

As you say this point your finger at the audience as if you're a parent telling your child something important.

The poor silversmith thanked him and came back the next day. He handed the spoon to the rich man and along with it a small silver spoon which looked **exactly** like the large one **except** for its size.

First, hold out one spoon with one hand and then the other spoon with your other hand.

The rich man looked at the two spoons and was puzzled. "Wait a minute. I lent you only the **large** spoon. Who owns this **small** spoon?"

Take your time with this part. Remember the rich man is confused and a bit suspicious. Look at the imaginary spoons in your hands as you say this.

"Why, it's **yours,**" replied the silversmith.

"Believe it or not, last night your big spoon **gave birth** to this **small** one. Because I am an honest man, I am returning both the mother ***and*** the baby to you."

Say this part as if you can't believe it yourself.

As you say "the mother" put out your right hand as if you were showing the audience the large spoon. Then as you say "the baby," put out your left hand.

The rich man thought this sounded **ridiculous,** but he was **too greedy** to argue with the silversmith. He **gladly** accepted **both** spoons.

Say this with uncertainty, but quickly change to greed and happiness as you say "but he was too greedy …"

A few days later, the silversmith returned to the rich man's house to borrow a large silver bowl. The rich man would **never** have considered lending something of such value to anyone else,

but he remembered what good
fortune he had had **last** time
he lent something to the
silversmith,
(pause)

As you say this, lean a bit toward the
audience, raise your eyebrows and look
greedy.

so he quickly agreed.

Say this quickly.

Two days passed,
and the silversmith returned
to the rich man again.
This time he carried **not only**
the rich man's **large** silver bowl
but also a **small** silver bowl,
identical in **every** way
except size.

Gesture with first the right hand and
then the left as if to show the two
bowls. Say this with amazement in your
voice.

"I know it's hard to believe,
but your **large bowl**
gave birth to a **tiny bowl.**
Since **both** of them
rightfully belong to **you,**
I am giving them to you now
so that my conscience will be
clear."

Again, say this part as if you are
astonished.

The rich man was **delighted,**
praised the silversmith for his
honesty, and **gladly** accepted the
two bowls.

As you say "gladly," make a gesture as if
to take the bowls greedily from
someone who is handing them to you.

Not too long after that the
silversmith returned **once again**
to the rich man and said,
"Would you mind lending me
your gold watch?"

The rich man didn't even hesitate. **"Why it would be my pleasure!"** He was, of course, thinking of the beautiful small watch that would be returned with it.

You must show a real change in the rich man at this point. In the beginning of the story he was suspicious. Now he is delighted to lend something to the silversmith since he thinks it will lead to more riches.

"Here, you may take my **finest** gold watch which is set with diamonds.
I am confident that you will return it to me
just as you promise.
And if it should happen
to have a child,
I have no doubt
that you will be **just** as honest
as you have been in the past."

Make a gesture as if to very enthusiastically hand the watch to the silversmith.

Say this as if you're talking to a good friend.

"Well, **of course,**"
said the silversmith,
and he went on his way.

One day passed,
and then another,
and still **another,**
but the rich man
saw **no sign** of the silversmith
and his gold watch.
Finally he grew **impatient**
and went to the silversmith's home.

Take a little pause after each comma in this sentence. This will help the audience feel the mounting tension that the rich man experiences while waiting for the return of his watch.

"I've come about my watch,"
the rich man asked politely.

The silversmith hung his head sadly and said, "I was planning to pay a visit to tell you the sad news. *(pause)*

Hang your head and try to sound extremely sad as you say this.

Last night your watch **died.**"

"Died?
You fool!
How can a watch die?"

The silversmith just smiled,
looked the rich man in the eye,
and said,
"If you believe that silver spoons
and bowls can **give birth,**
why should it surprise you
that a watch can **die?**"

And with that the silversmith
closed the door and went back to
his work, and the rich neighbor
returned home feeling **very**
foolish.

The rich man is not only very angry, but
he also cannot believe the silversmith's
words. Have a puzzled expression on
your face.

Don't rush this section. This story is a bit
like a joke and this part is the punch line.
Say this straight to the audience as if you
are teaching them a lesson.

After you say the last line of the story,
take a small step back and take a bow.

Why Anansi the Spider
Has a Small Waist

*A story from West Africa
retold by Martha Hamilton & Mitch Weiss
Beauty and the Beast Storytellers*

**This story about Anansi
(pronounced a -NON´ -see) the
spider is told in many countries
of West Africa. Anansi is a sly
trickster who often fools other
animals and people as well. Sometimes,
however, as in this story, Anansi gets into
trouble because of his ambitious plans.**

Nowadays,
if you look closely at a spider,
you will see
that he has a **big** head
and a **big** body
and a **tiny** waist in between.
But **long ago**
spiders **did not** have small waists.
I'll tell you the story
of how this came to be.

Make a big round circle with both hands
as you say "big head" and again when
you say "big body." Then make a
gesture to show a tiny waist.

Anansi the spider
LOVED to eat more than
anything. And he could smell
good cooking from a **mile** away.
One day when he was in the
forest he noticed
a **delicious** smell in the air.

Say this with a lot of enthusiasm.

Raise your eyebrows up and down a bit
and look as if you smell a delicious smell.

Sniff! Sniff! Sniff!
Where was the wonderful smell coming from?

Sniff in three different directions as if you're trying to find which direction the smell is coming from. Don't say the word "sniff" but instead pretend to actually sniff the air.

Just then Anansi remembered that today was the festival of the harvest.
The two villages nearby—
one to the **east,**
the other to the **west—**

Look as if you just had a brilliant idea.

Point to the right as you say "east" and to the left as you say "west."

would **both** be having feasts!
Anansi's mouth began to water.
He thought,

Look very excited as you say this. You could rub both hands together to show how pleased Anansi is.

"There will be **SO** much food!
I'll be able to eat
as much as I want!"
But,
Anansi wondered,
which village
would be serving the **best** food,
the one to the **east**
or the one to the **west?**

Get very excited and pat your stomach as you say this.

As you say "but," have a look of concern on your face.

Look confused as you say this.

Point to the right as you say "east" and to the left as you say "west."

Anansi thought,
"I'll go to BOTH feasts!
I'll find out
who will be serving food first.
I'll go there,
eat my fill,
and then go to the other village."

Get even more excited at the thought of *two* feasts.
Say this fast and excitedly. Try to show how brilliant Anansi thinks he is.

But
when Anansi went to
the two villages and asked
when the feasts would begin,
NO ONE would tell him.

Slowly

Sound very upset.

The people of **both** villages
knew that Anansi **never** did **any**
work to deserve a feast,
but **always** appeared
just when the food was served.

Say this with suspicion and disgust.

Anansi knew that if he showed
up, he could have
all the food he wanted
since it was the custom
of the villagers
not to refuse **anyone**
who came to their door hungry.

As you say "all," make a circular gesture with both hands.

Before long
Anansi came up
with what he **thought**
was a **VERY** clever plan.
First he called his eldest son.
Anansi tied a very long rope
around his **own** belly
and said to his son,

Again, look and sound as if you have a brilliant idea.

Pretend to tie a rope around your stomach as you say this.

"Take the other end of this rope
to the **east** village.
When the food is served,
give a **hard** pull
so that I'll know it's time
for me to come and eat."

Pretend to hand a rope to someone with both hands. Then point to the right as if pointing east.

Pretend to pull hard on a rope as you say this.

Then he called his youngest son.
Anansi took **another** long rope
and tied it around his belly also,
and told **that** son
to take the **other** end of the rope
toward the **west** village
and give a **hard** pull
when the food was ready.

Pretend to tie a rope around your stomach as you say this.

Pretend to hand a rope to someone with both hands. Then point to the left as if pointing west.

Pretend to pull hard on a rope as you say this.

Anansi **waited** and **waited** for the feasts to begin.	Say this as if you're very impatient.
Suddenly he felt a **hard pull** to the east. Anansi was **very** excited!	Say this quickly, with a lot of excitement. Jerk your waist to the right as you say "hard pull."
But just then	Slowly, with concern on your face.
there was a **hard pull** to the west.	Jerk your waist to the left as you say "hard pull," or at the end of the sentence.
Anansi realized that the **two villages** must have served their feasts at the **SAME TIME!**	Look very upset as you say this.
His two sons were **pulling SO** hard on their ropes that Anansi	As you say "pulling SO," make a pulling gesture with your hands, and show great strain in your voice.
was caught **RIGHT** in the middle.	Have a look of dread on your face.
He couldn't go to the **east** and he couldn't go to the **west.** The two sons kept pulling **as hard as they could** on their ropes until the feasts were **over** and **ALL** the food **was gone.**	Point to the right as you say "east" and to the left as you say "west." Say this with strain in your voice. Say this with great disappointment.
When they went to find their father to see why he hadn't come when they pulled, they found that he now had a **tiny** waist where the ropes had gone around his **big** belly. **And that is why** to **this** day **all** spiders have a **big** head and a **big** body and a **tiny little waist.**	Show great surprise on your face and in your voice as you say this. Make a big round circle with both hands as you say "big head" and again when you say "big body." Then make a gesture to show a tiny waist.

King Midas and the Golden Touch

A story from Greece
retold by
Martha Hamilton & Mitch Weiss
Beauty and the Beast Storytellers

**This Greek tale is one of the most
famous stories about greed. Before
you tell the story you could say to
your listeners, "If you could have
one wish, would it be for love, health,
happiness, peace on earth, or a big
house, lots of money, and anything you
wanted to buy? Here's what happened to
King Midas when he received his wish."**

Long ago in Greece
there lived a king named Midas.
He had **more gold** than **anyone**
in the world, but **still** it was not
enough. The **more** he had,
the **more** he wanted.

Look and sound very greedy as you say
this.

King Midas
had a flower garden,
(pause)

Point to the right as if to show the
flower garden to the audience.

but he did not spend much time
there. He also had a daughter
named Maragold whom he **loved
dearly**
(pause)

Point to the left as if to introduce
Maragold to the audience.

but he did not spend
much time with her either.
Instead he spent **many** hours of
the day in a vault **far** beneath his
palace **counting his gold.**

As you say "counting his gold," pretend to count gold coins greedily.

One day King Midas
was down in his treasure room
picking up **handfuls** of gold coins
and letting them slip through his
fingers.
Suddenly a stranger appeared
and said,
"My goodness, King Midas,
You **do** have a **lot** of gold!"

As you say this, pretend to pick up handfuls of gold and let them spill through your fingers.

Look very surprised and impressed as you say this.

Midas replied,
"But this gold is **nothing**
compared to **all** the gold in the
world."

As you say "nothing," look at the imaginary money with scorn, and then look very greedy as you say "all the gold in the world."

"You mean, you're not **satis-
fied?**" the stranger asked in a
surprised voice.

Show on your face and in your voice that the stranger finds this very hard to believe.

"Of course not," replied Midas.
"I am **always** trying
to think of ways to get **more** gold.
I wish that **everything** I touch
would turn to gold."

Continue to make Midas sound extremely greedy.

As you say "everything," make a gesture with both hands to show the audience how very greedy Midas is.

"Do you **really** wish that?" the
stranger asked.

Say this with disbelief.

"Of course, I wish it. **Nothing**
could make me happier!"

"Then you shall have your wish,"
said the stranger, and before
King Midas could **say** or **do**
anything, the stranger **vanished.**

As you say "vanished," make a quick movement with one hand, or snap your fingers.

King Midas couldn't wait
to see if it were **really** true.
He started to go upstairs to the
palace. But as he grabbed the
knob to open the door,
(pause)

Pause after you say "door" to create a little suspense. Say "the entire door turned to gold," with amazement.

the entire door turned to gold!

"It's true, it's true!" he shouted.

Look and sound very excited!

Midas was beside himself with
excitement thinking of **all** the
gold he could now have.

He **dashed** up the steps
to the palace
and ordered his servants
to prepare a feast to celebrate.

Say this quickly.

He sat down to eat,
and reached for a piece of bread.
(pause)
Instantly the **bread** turned to
gold.

As you say "reached for a piece of bread," pretend to do just that. Then pause, and show amazement and a little horror on your face before you say, "Instantly the bread turned to gold."

He took a glass of water in his
hand **but that, too,** became gold.

Pretend to pick up a glass of water and pause in the same way you did for the bread.

"Oh no!" he cried. "I'm **hungry**
and **thirsty** but I can't eat **gold.**"

Say this with despair.

Just then his daughter Maragold
walked into the room.

"What's the matter, Father?"
she asked as she ran to hug him.
But **just** as he picked her up
in his arms, he **cried out in horror.**
Maragold had changed
into a golden statue.
(pause)

With great horror in your voice and on your face.

King Midas realized
how foolish his wish had been.
He began to cry.

With sadness in your voice.

Just then the stranger
appeared and asked,
"King Midas, **aren't you happy**
now that you have the **golden**
touch?"

"No," replied Midas,
"for I have lost **all**
that was **worth having.**
Please **give me back my**
daughter, and I'll give up **all** the
gold I have!"

Again, with great sadness in your voice.

With desperation in your voice and on your face.

The stranger said,
"You are wiser
than you **were,** King Midas.
Go to the stream outside your
palace. Follow it **all the way**
into the mountains until you find
the place where the stream
begins.

Make a gesture with your hand as if to show the path up to the mountains.

Dip yourself in the river and that
will take away your golden
touch. Then bring back a pitcher
of the water and sprinkle it on

your daughter
and anything else that you wish
to change back as it was."

With that, the stranger **disappeared.**   Again, make a quick motion with one
hand to show the disappearance.

King Midas did as he was told.
After he dipped himself in the
water, he was no longer able
to turn things into gold
by touching them.
He carried a pitcher of water
all the way back to the palace.
As soon as he sprinkled it on
Maragold, she **began to change.**   With amazement at first and then joy.
At first **her color returned.**
Then **her eyes opened,**
and her arms **reached out**
toward her father.

King Midas hugged Maragold
with tears rolling down his
cheeks.

He **now** understood
that his love for Maragold
outshone **all** of his gold.
From then on
he was a wise and generous ruler
who liked to warn others,
"Watch out what you wish for.   Don't rush the ending.
It just **might** come true."

Most Challenging Stories

The Mirror That Caused Trouble

A story from Korea
retold by Martha Hamilton & Mitch Weiss
Beauty and the Beast Storytellers

There are many stories told in the Far East about mirrors, many of them from a time long ago when most people had never seen one. To tell this story well, concentrate on the expression on your face. Practice with a mirror to see how you're doing.

Long ago
a young Korean farmer named
Kim
lived with his family
way out in the country.

Make a hand gesture to show that it is far away as you say "way out in the country."

One day Kim
went to the city of Seoul
on business.
He had never left
his little village before
and was **amazed**
by the sights of Seoul.
So many people,
so many goods for sale!

Seoul is pronounced just like the word "soul."

Look toward the audience with amazement, as if you are seeing the sights of a big city for the first time. If you look as if you are seeing these things, the audience will picture them in their minds easily.

In one shop he picked up a
small, round shiny object and
looked at it.
(pause)

As you say this, pretend to pick up a
mirror and then look at your open palm
as if you are holding the mirror in it.
During the pause, show a look of
surprise on your face right after Kim
looks in the mirror.

He was **surprised** to see a man
staring **right** back at him!

Say this with a feeling of amazement in
your voice.

Kim smiled—

While still holding your palm in front of
you, smile into the imaginary mirror.

and the man smiled back!

Look and sound very surprised, almost
shocked, as you say "and the man smiled
back."

Kim wrinkled his forehead—

Frown into the imaginary mirror.

and so did the man!

Again, look very surprised.

Kim didn't realize it was a mirror
since at that time most people
who lived in a small village
had never seen one before.
He was **so** amused by it
that he bought one for himself.

Don't forget to say this or the story will
not make sense.

When he returned home
he gave his family gifts
and entertained them **for hours**
with stories about the big city.

The next morning, however,
while Kim was out in the fields,
his wife, Cho, found the mirror.

She picked it up, looked at it,
and began to cry.

Pretend to pick up and hold the
imaginary mirror in your palm. Look and
sound very upset as you say "and began
to cry."

Kim's parents lived with them
and just at that moment his
mother walked into the room.
"Cho, what's the matter?"

Sound very concerned.

"Just look," Cho replied,
handing her mother-in-law
the mirror.
"Kim has brought home
a **beautiful young** woman
from Seoul to take my place."

As you say "Just look," point toward the imaginary mirror in your hand.
Sound very upset as you pretend to hand the mirror to the mother-in-law.

"Let me see," said Kim's mother.
She looked into the mirror
and laughed out loud.

Pretend to look into the mirror. You can either say "and laughed out loud" with laughter in your voice OR you can say nothing and laugh instead.

"**Cho, there must be something
wrong with your eyes!**
This is no **young** woman.
She's **old** and **not** very good
looking."

Say this as if you think Cho has gone crazy.

As you say this, point to the imaginary mirror in your palm and pretend to show it to the audience.

The two women
passed the mirror back and forth,
arguing about what they saw.

Make a hand gesture to show the back and forth movement.

It was then
that Kim's father entered the room.
He saw his daughter-in-law crying
and his wife laughing, and said,
"What's going on here?"

Pretend to see the daughter-in-law on your right and then the wife on your left. Look and sound very confused.

Each explained **her** side of the story.
"Let **me** see it. **I'll** settle this,"
said the father-in-law, and he
picked up the mirror and looked at it.

Point to yourself as you say "I'll."

Look at the imaginary mirror in your palm and have a very puzzled look on your face.

"**Have you two lost your minds?**
My son hasn't brought home a
woman, either young **or** old.
It's an **old man** with a **bald head!**"

Say this with feeling; Kim's father thinks they've gone crazy.

Point to the imaginary mirror in your palm as you say "It's an old man with a bald head."

They **argued** and **argued.**
The daughter insisted
she saw a **young woman,**
the mother-in-law an **old woman,**
and the father-in-law an **old man.**

Make a hand gesture toward the right,
then in front of you, and then to the left
as you mention each character.

None of them could convince the
others that they were wrong.
At last they put the mirror down
and went off to do their chores.

Pretend to put the mirror down.

Kim and Cho had a young son
who was happily playing
with a paper dragon
his father had brought
from Seoul.
He discovered the mirror
and looked into it.

Pretend to put the mirror in your palm
and look into it.

He thought he saw **another** boy
with **his** paper dragon.
**"Hey, who said YOU could
play with MY dragon? Give it
back right now!"**

Look at your palm and say this very
angrily.

Just then Kim came back to the
house and hearing this, said,

Because you look at the mirror a lot in
this story, be sure to look at the
audience when you are being the
narrator.

"Who's taken your dragon?"

With anger!

His son handed the mirror to him
and Kim looked into it.
**"What kind of man are you?
Stealing from little children!!
I'll teach you a lesson."**

Again, look into the imaginary mirror
and say this with even more anger.

And with that Kim gave the man
in the mirror a **big PUNCH.**

Pretend to punch the mirror as you say
"PUNCH."

The glass shattered **all** over
the floor!

Look toward the floor and gesture with
both hands to show where the glass
shattered.

And that was the end of the
mirror that caused trouble.

The Paper Bag Princess

A story by Robert N. Munsch

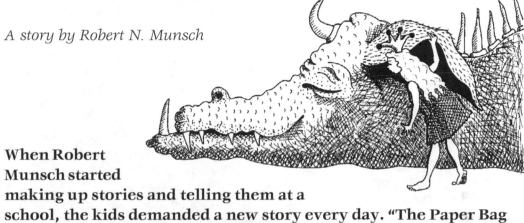

When Robert Munsch started making up stories and telling them at a school, the kids demanded a new story every day. "The Paper Bag Princess" was story number 219! If you haven't read his many books or heard him on cassette, make a trip to your local bookstore or library.

Elizabeth was a **beautiful** princess. She lived in a castle and had **expensive** princess clothes. She was going to marry a prince named Ronald

As you say "expensive princess clothes," use both hands to point from your shoulders down toward your feet as if to show off your clothes.

Unfortunately, a dragon **smashed** her castle,

Make a karate chop gesture as you say "smashed."

burned **all** her clothes with his **fiery** breath,

As you say "all her clothes," point with both hands from your shoulders down toward your feet, but this time have a look of disgust on your face.

and **carried off** Prince Ronald.

As you say "carried off," make a motion with one hand starting from your chest and going out toward the audience.

Elizabeth decided to **chase** the dragon and get Ronald back.

Say this sentence with great determination in your voice.

117

She looked **everywhere**
for something to wear

Look all around.

but the **only** thing she could find
that was **not** burnt
was a paper bag.

Shrug your shoulders as you say "was a
paper bag."

So she **put on** the paper bag

As you say "put on the paper bag," use
both hands to point toward your
shoulders and then downward.

and **followed** the dragon.

As you say "followed," use one hand to
make a gesture from your chest toward
the audience.

He was easy to follow
because he left a trail
of **burnt** forests and horses' **bones.**

Look revolted as you say "burnt forests
and horses' bones."

Finally Elizabeth came to a cave
with a large door
that had a **huge** knocker on it.
She took hold of the knocker
and **banged** on the door.

Pretend to lift a very heavy knocker and
bang it against a door.

The dragon **stuck** his nose
out of the door and said,

Say this very grumpily, with a disgusted
look on your face.

"**Well, a princess!**
I love to eat princesses,

Change quickly to a look of excitement.
Rub your hands together. Make your
voice as deep as you can for the dragon.

but I have already eaten
a **whole** castle today.
I am a **very** busy dragon.
Come back tomorrow."

Go back to sounding grumpy as the
dragon realizes Elizabeth is of no use to
him right now.

He **slammed** the door **so** fast
that Elizabeth almost
got her nose caught.

As you say "slammed," pretend to slam
a door. As you say "almost got her nose
caught," move your head and upper
body slightly backward and look very
upset.

Elizabeth **grabbed** the knocker
and **banged** on the door **again.**

Pretend to do this as before, but with a little more force because Elizabeth is even more determined now.

The dragon **stuck** his nose
out of the door and said,

"**Go AWAY.** I love to eat princesses,
but I have already eaten
a **whole** castle today.
I am a **very** busy dragon.
Come back **tomorrow.**"

Keep the same deep dragon's voice but sound even more annoyed.

"**Wait,**" shouted Elizabeth.
"Is it **true**
that you are the **smartest**
and **fiercest** dragon
in the **whole** world?"

Elizabeth has quickly come up with a plan to tell the dragon how great he is so that she can get what she wants from him. Have a look of wonder in your voice and on your face as you say this.

"**Yes,**" said the dragon.

Before you speak as the dragon, hold your shoulders and head up high and then say "Yes," in a proud, snooty way.

"Is it **true,**" said Elizabeth,
that you can burn up **ten** forests
with your **fiery** breath?"

Say this with great wonder and amazement as well.

"Oh, **yes,**" said the dragon,

Again, make your body look like a proud, snooty dragon before you speak.

and he took a **huge, deep** breath

When you say "huge, deep," make it sound as if what the dragon is doing requires a lot of effort. As you say "so," make a fast motion with both hands starting from your mouth and going out toward the audience.

and breathed out **so** much fire

that he burnt up **50** forests.

Say this with great amazement.

"**Fantastic,**" said Elizabeth,

Sound very excited.

and the dragon took
another **HUGE** breath,

Really stretch out the word "huge."

and breathed out **SO** much fire
that he burnt up
100 forests.

Say this with even more amazement
than before.

"Magnificent," said Elizabeth

Sound very excited.

and the dragon took
another **HUGE** breath,
(pause)

but this time **nothing** came out.
The dragon didn't even have
enough fire left to cook
a **meat ball.**

Sound very disappointed.

Elizabeth said,
"Dragon, is it **true**
that you can fly around the world
in just **ten** seconds?"

With great wonder in your voice and on
your face. Remember, Elizabeth is
flattering the dragon to trick him.

"Why, yes," said the dragon
and **jumped** up and **flew**

Be sure to get into your dragon pose
before speaking.

ALL the way around the world
in just **TEN** seconds.

Make a large circular motion with one
hand as you say "all the way around the
world."

He was **very** tired when he got
back, but Elizabeth shouted,

Sound tired.

"Fantastic, do it again!"

Say this with great energy.

So the dragon **jumped** up and
flew around the whole world
in just **20** seconds.

Make the same circular motion.

When he got back
he was **too tired to talk**

Sound very tired.

and he lay down
and went straight to sleep.
Elizabeth whispered **very** softly,
"Hey, dragon."
(pause)

Say this in a whispery voice but loud
enough for everyone to hear.
As you pause, pretend to look at the
dragon lying on the ground in front of
you.

The dragon didn't move at **all.**
She lifted up the dragon's ear
and put her head right inside.
She shouted as loud as she could,
"HEY, DRAGON!"

Pretend to lift up an enormous ear and
put your head inside.

Say this very loudly!

The dragon was **so** tired
he didn't even **move.**
Elizabeth walked
right over the dragon
and opened the door to the cave.
THERE was Prince Ronald.

Look and sound very excited as you
point to a place just above the heads of
the audience and pretend to see Prince
Ronald.

He looked at her and said,
"Elizabeth, you are a **mess!**
You **smell** like ashes,
your hair is **all** tangled,
and you are wearing
a **dirty old paper bag.**
Come back
when you are dressed
like a **real** princess."

Change to a look of disgust on your
face and in your voice as Ronald speaks,
and make him sound very snooty.

"Ronald," said Elizabeth,
"your clothes are **really** pretty
and your hair is **very** neat.
You look like a **real** prince,
but **YOU** are a **BUM!"**
(pause)

Put your hands on your hips before
Elizabeth begins to speak. Sound as if
you are angry but you are trying very
hard to control it. Then let all the anger
come out when you say "you are a
bum!"

They **didn't** get married after **all.**

Who Will Close the Door?

A story from India retold by Martha Hamilton & Mitch Weiss Beauty and the Beast Storytellers

Much of this story consists of dialogue between a husband and a wife. We have omitted the continual repetition of "he said, she said" that can be awkward when a story is told orally. Instead you will need to show with body language that two different people are speaking. One technique is to choose a way of holding your body for each character. For example, you could put your hands on your hips and lean slightly forward for the wife and hold your shoulders high or fold your arms across your chest for the husband.

There once lived a husband and wife who were both **extremely** stubborn. One evening after dinner they were sitting in their living room when a cold gust of wind **blew** their front door open.

As you say "blew," make a movement with one hand starting from your chest and moving quickly toward the audience to suggest the door being blown open.

"Wife, shut the door!" shouted the husband.

Hold your shoulders high or fold your arms across your chest. Say this in a very firm voice.

122

"**Husband, shut it** yourself!"
his wife answered.

Put your hands on your hips and lean slightly forward. Say this in an equally firm voice.

"**I** didn't open it,
and **I** won't shut it!" *(husband)*

Hold your shoulders high or fold your arms across your chest. Make your voice more and more angry as the argument continues.

"**I** didn't open it either,
and I'll **certainly** not shut it!"
(wife)

Put your hands on your hips and lean slightly forward.

They both **folded** their arms
over their chests and sat in silence
fuming over the fact
that the **other** one
would **not** get up and **shut** the door.

Fold your arms and look extremely upset.

The icy wind **howled.**

Unfold your arms.

The storm **swirled** about their cottage.

Make a circular motion with your hand to show the swirling of the wind.

But the couple just **sat there,**
their teeth chattering

Fold your arms across your chest again as you say "sat there."

and their fingers turning blue
from the cold.

Rub your hands together to show how cold they are.

"**Wife,** I've worked hard
all day long in the fields.
I need my rest, **please,**
shut the door." *(husband)*

Hold your shoulders high or fold your arms across your chest.

"Do you think the house was
cleaned, the cows milked, **and** the
supper cooked while I was lying
down? My feet are tired,
you get up and shut the door!"
(wife)

Put your hands on your hips and lean slightly forward. Sound angry.

Point to audience members as if they are the husband as you say "you."

123

Both of them knew that this
argument could go on **forever.**
Finally, in the hope
of putting an end to it,
the man said,
"All right! **You** didn't open it,
and **I** didn't open it.
You don't want to get up,
and **I** don't want to get up.
Let's make a pact.
You and I will sit here
until one of us speaks.
Whoever speaks first will **have**
to get up and **shut the door!**"

Hold your shoulders high or fold your arms across your chest. Point to yourself each time you say "I" and toward the audience as you say "you."

"That suits me **just** fine!" *(wife)*

Put your hands on your hips and lean slightly forward.

They both got comfortable on
their stools and sat in silence.

Fold your arms across your chest and look very stubborn.

The two of them had been **so**
caught up in their argument
that they did not see a stranger
lurking outside their front door.
This man, who was a thief,
had walked by and seen
their front door standing **wide** open.
After overhearing their argument
and the bet they had made,
he was convinced that
he would profit from **their** stupidity.

Unfold your arms and speak directly to the audience.

Point to yourself as you say "he" and toward the audience as you say "their."

He walked in **boldly** and stood
right in the middle of the room.

Gesture toward the middle of the audience with your hand as you say "right."

Neither the wife **nor** the husband
said a word.

Show surprise in your voice and on your face as you say this.

The thief thought to himself,
"This is going to be easier than I
thought. These two must be
crazy!"
He noticed a jar of cookies
on the table so he took off the lid
and helped himself to one.

Lean a bit closer toward the audience and say this as if you are letting them in on a secret. Point to the imaginary husband and wife as you say "These two must be crazy!"

Pretend to see the jar of cookies. Pointing at it with your finger will help you to focus your eyes on it.

Neither the man **nor** the woman
said a word.
Since the cookie was delicious
and the jar was **full** of them,
he put the **whole jar** in his sack.
He went around the cottage taking
what he could find, even though
nothing was of very much value—
an old tattered coat, a cooking pot,
a ragged quilt from the bed.

Say this with disbelief.

Pretend to put the jar in a sack.

Gesture with your hands toward these objects as you pretend to see them with your eyes. Sound very disappointed as you mention these objects.

"Just my luck!"
he thought to himself.
"I find two people who will **sit**
and let me take **anything** that I
want, and wouldn't you know it?
There's **nothing worth taking!**"

Say this with disgust in your voice.

Put both hands out to your sides to show total frustration.

Just then he opened
a chest of drawers and found
a **beautifully** carved wooden box.
This was the **only** thing of value
that the couple owned.
It contained the little money
they had to their names.
As the thief picked up the box,
the husband and wife
both **JUMPED** up
and at **exactly** the same time,
shouted,
"Don't you dare touch that!"

Gesture as if you are opening a chest of drawers and then pretend to see the box.

Pretend to pick up the box.

As you say "JUMPED," make a slight jolting motion with your body.

Point right toward the audience as you shout this. Look at everyone, not just one person.

The thief was so **startled** by this sudden response that he	As you say "startled," go slightly backward with a jolting motion in your head and upper body.
grabbed his sack	Pretend to grab a sack as you say "grabbed."
and **bolted** out the door.	As you say "bolted," make a quick motion with one hand starting from your chest and going out toward the audience as if to show him tearing down the road.
But neither the husband **nor** the wife set out after him. Instead the husband turned to his wife: "**You** spoke first, so go and **shut** the door."	Hold your shoulders high or fold your arms across your chest. Point to the imaginary wife as you say "you."
"**What!! You** were the first to speak, so **you** shut it!" *(wife)*	Put your hands on your hips and lean slightly forward.
"Not on your life!" *(husband)*	Hold your shoulders high or fold your arms across your chest.
"Admit it. **You** lost, **you** shut it." *(wife)*	Put your hands on your hips and lean slightly forward.
	The rest of the arguing should go fairly quickly back and forth.
"YOU SHUT IT!!"*(husband)*	Hold your shoulders high or fold your arms across your chest.
"YOU SHUT IT!!" *(wife)*	Put your hands on your hips and lean slightly forward.
"YOU SHUT IT!!" *(husband)*	Hold your shoulders high or fold your arms across your chest.
They **may** have settled their argument by now, but on the other hand, that door may **yet** be open, because the last *I* heard, they were **STILL** arguing.	Say the last sentence slowly.

The Stonecutter

*A story from Japan
retold by Martha Hamilton &
Mitch Weiss
Beauty and the Beast
Storytellers*

**This story is a circle story,
meaning it ends up in the same place it began. It's a
thoughtful story, the kind that draws people in and really makes
them listen.**

In Japan **long** ago
there lived a stonecutter
who went **every** day
to the side of a mountain.
There he chipped away
at the rock
with his mallet and chisel.
He sold **big** slabs of rock
for gravestones
or to build houses.
He was happy with his work,
and never thought he wanted
anything more.

Gesture as if to chip at the rock.

As you say "big," hold both hands out
to the side to show the large size of the
rock.

But **one** day the stonecutter
delivered stone
to the house of a **very** rich man.
There he saw
all sorts of **beautiful** things,
things which he had never
even **dreamed of.**

Say "But one day" slowly. This is when things begin to change for the stonecutter.

Say this with envy in your voice.

The next day his work
seemed **harder.**
His chisel and mallet
seemed **heavier.**

Lower your shoulders a bit and say this as if you're doing something that requires a lot of effort.

He thought to himself,
"If only I were a RICH MAN!"

This line will repeat (with a different ending) throughout the story. Say it with a feeling of greed and envy each time. Putting both hands in front of you and using them to emphasize "rich man" will add to the effect.

His wish was heard
by the spirit
who lived in the mountain.
That evening,
when the stonecutter
returned to his little hut,
(pause)

he saw instead **a beautiful palace!**

Right after you say "returned to his little hut," have a look of shock and amazement on your face as you pretend to see the palace in front of you. This keeps the audience in suspense for a second. Afterward say, with great excitement, "he saw instead a beautiful palace!"

He slept that night
in a **huge** bed with a **golden**
canopy.
In the morning
he gazed out the window
as he ate the breakfast
his servants
had brought to him in bed.

Hold your head up a little higher during this part; say it as if he's living a grand life.

Down on the street
he saw **a great procession.**
There was the **king,**
being carried on a **pedestal**
by his servants and soldiers.
The stonecutter thought,
"If only I were the KING!"

As you say "being carried on a pedestal," gesture with your hand upward and to the side to show that the king is above everyone.

With a feeling of greed and envy.

The mountain spirit heard him.

Suddenly the stonecutter was
dressed in robes
of the **finest** silk,

Say this with amazement. As you say "robes of the finest silk," make a gesture with both hands from your shoulders and down your body as if to show the clothes.

being carried aloft through the town.

Again, gesture with your hand upward and to the side to show that the stonecutter is now above everyone. Pretend to look at him as he passes by.

He was now
the most **powerful** person
in the land.

Hold your shoulders and head high as you say this.

He was quite happy
until one day,
as he walked in the royal garden,
he noticed that his flowers
were being **scorched** by the sun.

Point toward the ground with a disturbed look on your face as you say "his flowers were being scorched by the sun."

The stonecutter was **outraged:**
"No matter **how much** I take
care of these flowers,
the **sun's** power is by **far** greater.
If only I were the SUN!"

Sound outraged!

Look up toward the sun. The feeling of greed and anger in your voice should be a little stronger each time you make a wish.

With a **flash** of light
the mountain spirit
turned the stonecutter
into the sun.

As you say "flash," make a quick upward motion with both hands OR snap your fingers.

He could look out
over the **entire** world.

As you say "over the entire world," hold both hands, palms down, in front of your chest. Make a circular motion going toward the audience and then to both sides.

To show his great might
he shone down on the earth
with **blistering** hot rays.
Day after day
he **burned** the farmers' fields
and **dried up** the rivers.

Make the sun sound very powerful, but also cruel.

Then one day a cloud
covered the sun.
Its rays could no longer
reach the earth.
The stonecutter thought,
"Is it possible that the **cloud** is
even **stronger** than the **sun?**

Say this with a feeling of disbelief.

If only I were a CLOUD!"

Say this with even more greed.

No **sooner**
had he spoken these words
than the mountain spirit
turned him into a cloud.
He could now
block the sun's **powerful** rays.
Before long the earth
was once again green.
Flowers **bloomed,**

Remember to have a sense of wonder in your voice each time the stonecutter changes.

As you say "block," hold both hands up as if you're telling someone to stop.

As you say "flowers bloomed," put both hands in front of you, palms up, and make an upward motion.

and the rivers **flowed** with water.

As you say "flowed," use both hands to make a gesture like a river flowing downstream.

But the stonecutter
was **overcome** by his new power.
He began to **rain** and **rain** and **rain.**
Towns and villages were **destroyed.**
All that remained
was the great mountain.

As you say "destroyed," use one hand, palm down, to make a gesture from your chest to the side. Freeze your hand to the side until you say "was the great mountain." Then turn your palm upward and point toward an imaginary mountain in the distance.

The stonecutter was **astonished.**
"Everything has been **washed away** by the force of **my** rain.

Say this with great pride. As you say "washed away," make a quick motion with one hand from in front of your chest out toward the audience.

Except for the **mountain!**

Look and sound angry as you say "except for the mountain."

Perhaps the **mountain**
is even stronger than the **cloud.**
**If only I were
the MOUNTAIN!"**
The mountain spirit
heard his wish
and turned the stonecutter
into the mountain.
Proudly he stood.
The **hot** rays of the sun
and the **force** of the rain
had **no** effect on him.

As you say this, change quickly from anger to a feeling of greed. Make this wish the most dramatic—he's almost crazy with greed by now.

Stand tall and straight. Show how the stonecutter now feels that nothing can hurt him.

But one day
he heard a **strange** noise
at his feet.
He looked down
to see what it could be.
He saw a man raise his hammer
and strike him.

Have a confused look on your face to show that the stonecutter doesn't understand what's happening.

Pretend to raise a hammer and strike at the mountain as you say this.

He felt the blow
all through his stony body.

As you say "all through his stony body," make a gesture with both hands from your shoulders and down your body.

At last a great piece of rock
broke off
and **fell** to the ground.

As you say "broke off," make a karate chop motion with one hand. Freeze your hand in that position until you say "fell," and then make a downward motion.

A **chill** swept through him
as he realized
that the **stonecutter**
was the **strongest of all.**

Scrunch up your shoulders and let a bit of a chill sweep through your body as you say "chill."

This is a very powerful ending when done slowly and with feeling.

Wait Till Whalem-Balem Comes

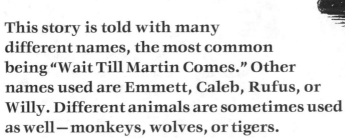

*An African-American
folktale
retold by Martha Hamilton
& Mitch Weiss
Beauty and the Beast
Storytellers*

**This story is told with many
different names, the most common
being "Wait Till Martin Comes." Other
names used are Emmett, Caleb, Rufus, or
Willy. Different animals are sometimes used
as well—monkeys, wolves, or tigers.**

**We have written this story in a form to be
told by two tellers (A and B), although it can
also be told by one person. If you do choose a partner, be sure it's
one with whom you work very well.**

A: Late one night
a man was walking home,
and a **big** storm came up.
The rain **poured** down in **buckets.**
The wind **swirled** so **hard**
he could barely walk.
He **knew** he would **have** to find
a place to stay for the night.
He'd **never** make it home
in **this** weather.

Try to set a spooky tone right from the
first sentence.

As you say "swirled," make the
following movement: put both hands to
your left, at about chest height, and
move them quickly to the right.

132

B: BUT the only shelter nearby
was an old deserted house
just down the road.
People said
the house was haunted.
Just thinking
of the stories he'd heard,
made the hair on his neck rise.

Say this slowly with a scared look on your face.

As you say "made the hair on his neck rise," scrunch up your shoulders and look frightened.

A: BUT he didn't really
have a choice.
So he ran as **fast** as he could
toward the house.

Speed up as you say this sentence.

He put his hand to the door
handle, opened the door,

Slow down as you say this to show that the man is nervous. Pretend to open a door very slowly, and look worried about what you might find inside.

CREEEEEEEEAK!

Both tellers could do the creaky noise if you find that sounds best.

and stepped into the hallway.
(pause)

During the pause, pretend to look around the hallway.

But just then

Say this quickly. Keep your head facing forward, but show with your eyes that you are trying to see what's behind you. Look very afraid.

CREEEEEEEEEAK!

Do this slowly.

Both A and B: SLAM!

Instead of saying "SLAM!" you could stomp your feet and clap your hands at the same time to make a loud noise.

(pause)

During the pause, turn your head slowly and look back as if to see what made the noise. Look very worried.

A: the door **slammed shut**
behind him!

Say this with a look on your face that says "Uh-oh. This place really must be haunted."

B: (sigh) "It's going to be a **very** long night."

Say this with the same worried look. The sigh at the beginning gives the feeling that he realizes there's nothing he can do about it—he's stuck there for the night.

A: The house sure was **big** and **dark.**

Look around and pretend to see how big and dark it looks.

B: There were spider webs **everywhere.**

Pretend to see the spider webs. Have a look of disgust on your face.

A: He made a fire
to shake the **chill**
he'd gotten from the **cold** rain.
He pulled up a chair
right by the fire,
took the newspaper
out of his bag,
and began to read.

Shake your shoulders and let a little chill run through your body as you say this.

Pretend to read a newspaper you are holding in front of you with both hands.

B: Suddenly
he heard a **strange** noise.

He looked up to find
a **large** black cat
STARING at him.

Say "Suddenly" quickly, but then slow down. Look around as if you are nervously listening to try and figure out what the noise was.

Point straight ahead and pretend to see the eyes staring at you. Look worried.

B: It sat **perfectly** still
and looked at the man
with **fiery** eyes.

Look and sound mean as you say "fiery."

This was **no ordinary** house cat.
The man thought it best
to ignore the cat,
so he buried his head
in his newspaper.

Look and sound very nervous as you say "This was no ordinary house cat."

Pretend to hold a newspaper in front of you. Scrunch your shoulders and move both hands upward as if you are hiding behind the newspaper. Keep your hands out to the side so the audience can see your face.

A: When he finally
got the nerve to look up
there were **two** sets of eyes
staring at him.

Again, point straight ahead and pretend to see the eyes staring at you. Look and sound a bit more worried.

B: The second set
belonged to a **huge** black cat,

Both tellers should pretend to see an enormous black cat.

Both A and B:
as big as a DOG.

It will take a lot of practice to be able to say this together well. If it ends up being too hard, teller B can say it.

A: Just then the first cat
looked at the other one and said,
"What do you think
we should DO with him?"

Before you say "What do you think we should DO with him?" hold your shoulders high and get a real tough, mean look on your face.

B: The huge black cat replied,
"Wait till **Whalem-Balem** comes."

Say this slowly, and in a very mischievous way.

A: The man kept on reading
but his hands were **shaking,**
and his heart was **racing.**
Again he felt **more** eyes upon
him, and when he looked up
there was a third
FIERCE-looking cat,

As you say this, pretend to hold the newspaper up in front of you, but this time look very nervous and shake your hands a bit.

Both tellers should have a look of horror on your faces as you pretend to see the cat.

Both A and B:
as big as a CALF!

Say this like you can't believe it, and at the same time show that the man is scared.

A: The first cat turned
to the others,
pointed right at the man,
and said,
"What do you think
we should DO with him?"

You might want to rub your hands together to show you're up to no good.

B: "Wait till
Whalem-Balem comes."

Again, say this slowly and mischievously.

A: Once again the man
buried his head in his newspaper,
although by this time

Pretend to read the newspaper once again, but this time look and sound as if you're terrified.

he was **so** scared that he couldn't
make out any of the words.
He broke out into a **cold sweat.**

B: It wasn't long before the man
felt **another** set of eyes
staring at him.
The others had been joined
by a **monstrous** black cat,

When you say "monstrous," have a
horrified look on your face.

Both A and B:
as big as a HORSE.

Let your eyes get really big as you
pretend to see the cat. Say this with
shock and great terror.

A: Again the first cat
looked **right** at the man:
"What do you think
we should DO with him?"

Again, make yourself look tough and
threatening as you say this.

B: "Wait till
Whalem-Balem comes."

Say this slowly. Rub your hands together
and sound evil.

A: That man had no idea
WHO or **WHAT**
Whalem-Balem was,
but he **knew**
he did **NOT** want to meet him.

Sound very upset and scared. Gesture to
the right as you say "who" and to the
left as you say "what."

As you say "not," put your hand in front
of you at chest level. Move it forcefully
from left to right.

He **jumped** up,
bolted out the door
and shouted,
"When Whalem-Balem comes,
you tell **HIM** that **I** couldn't wait."

Say this part very quickly. Make
appropriate hand movements as you say
"jumped" and "bolted."

As you say "HIM," point toward the
audience. As you say "I," point toward
yourself.

B: The man **tore** down the road

Both A and B:
like a **streak of lightning**

Say this very quickly. You (both tellers)
may want to put your hands in front of
you at waist level and move them
rapidly from left to right as you say this.

B: and if Whalem-Balem
ever **did** come,
you can be **sure**
that man **wasn't** there.

Say this part slowly.

Whalem-Balem never actually arrives during the story. At the end listeners may ask, "What was Whalem-Balem?" In answer, ask them, "What did YOU think it was?" There are no wrong answers. Audience members see different pictures in their minds while listening to stories. Some may have thought Whalem-Balem was a cat as big as an elephant, others an evil man who was the owner of the cats. Still others may say they thought Whalem-Balem was only a mouse, or nothing at all, and the cats were just trying to trick the man into thinking something horrible was coming.

Master of All Masters

A story from England retold by Martha Hamilton & Mitch Weiss Beauty and the Beast Storytellers

We have written this story in a form to be told by two tellers (A and B), although it can also be told by one person. If you do choose a partner, be sure it's one with whom you work very well.

    Much of this story consists of dialogue between Mr. Fusselbudget and the young woman. We have omitted the continual repetition of "he said, she said" that can be awkward when a story is told orally. Depending on the sex of the tellers and the roles you wish to play, you could, for example, change the characters to Mrs. Fusselbudget or a young man.

A: Long ago
in a small village in England
there lived a young woman
who one day went to town
to try and find work as a house-
keeper.
She **finally** talked with
a **strange**-looking gentleman
named Mr. Fusselbudget.
He agreed to hire her,
but as soon as they got back
to his house, he sat her down
and had a talk with her.

As you say "a strange-looking gentleman," have a strange look on your face, and point toward your partner.

Since Mr. Fusselbudget is a bit odd, you might want to have a funny voice for him. If you do you must remember to change your voice each time he talks. Bending over a bit and pointing toward your partner as if you're trying to teach her a lesson also works well.

B: "Now if you're going to live here and clean and cook for me, there are some things
I must teach you,
for in **my** house
I have my own names for
everything!"

Point to yourself as you say "in my house."

A: "Yes, sir."

The young woman is very patient and obedient at the beginning of the story and gradually loses her patience.

B: "Now, what will you call **me?**"

Point to yourself as you say "me."

A: "Why, Mr. Fusselbudget, sir."

B: "**NO**—around here I like to be called '**Master of all Masters.**'"

Sound very important as you say this.

A: "Yes sir, why of course, sir."

At this point the young woman is still very polite, although she's beginning to realize that Mr. Fusselbudget is a bit strange.

B: Next he pointed to his bed. "And what would you call **this?**"

Point to an imaginary bed.

A: "Why, that is a **bed**, sir."

Look toward the spot where your partner pointed and pretend to see the bed.

B: "No, that's my **bumper rumper.**"

You may wish to nod your head with a jolting movement when Mr. Fusselbudget says "bumper rumper," and each time he says one of his funny names.

A: "Yes, if you say so, sir."

Look very polite as you turn toward Mr. Fusselbudget to say this, but afterward give the audience a look as if to say "This man is out of his mind!"

B: "And what do you call **these?**"

Point to your pants as you say this. (If you aren't wearing pants, pretend you are.)

A: "Let's see, those are pants or trousers or breeches, sir."

B: "**NO! Nothing of the kind!**
These are my **rowser bowsers.**"

Mr. Fusselbudget is beginning to lose his patience.

A: "I'll **try** to remember that, sir."

Say this with sarcasm in your voice OR give the audience another look as if to say "This man is crazy!"

B: "I **EXPECT** that you will!"
Then Mr. Fusselbudget
pointed to his cat.
"And what about **her**?
What name would you have for **her?**"

Sound very annoyed.

Point to an imaginary cat.

A: "**Most** people would call her a cat or kitten, sir."

Be sure to look at the imaginary cat your partner has pointed to.

B: "**Not I!** I call her the
'**white-whiskered wonder**'
and **so** must **YOU!**"

Point to yourself as you say "Not I!"
Point to your partner as you say "you."

A: "By all means, sir, whatever you say." *(sigh)*

A big sigh after you say this would show that the young woman is now beginning to lose her patience.

B: "And **this,**" he said,
as he pointed to the fire,
"**this** is a **scorchablazintorch.**"

Point to an imaginary fire.

A: "Well, sir, you could have fooled me. **I** thought it was a fire."

Look at the imaginary fire with shock and say this with great sarcasm.

B: "**ENOUGH of your talk, just remember it!**"

Sound extremely annoyed.

A: "Yes, sir."

B: Mr Fusselbudget held up a bucket. "And **now,** what about **this?**"

Hold up an imaginary bucket.

A: "Why, I'd call that a pail or bucket, sir."

B: "Not around here, you
won't. This is a puddle ruddle!"

A: "If you insist, sir."

B: "I DO!"
"**Surely** you must know what
this is," said Mr. Fusselbudget
while showing her the water in
the bucket.

Pretend to show your partner what's in
the bucket.

A: "Water, or wet, or **WHAT-
EVER YOU PLEASE SIR!**"

Sound and look as if you are extremely
frustrated.

B: "No! No! No! This is
pondalorum.

Shake both arms and stomp one foot as
you say "No! No! No!" to show how
upset you are with her.

Now, **last** but not **least,** what
would you call **this?**"

Make a broad gesture with your hand as
if to point to an imaginary house.

A: "Why it's a house or cottage,
sir."

Look up and pretend to see the house.

B: "**NO!** Listen carefully—you
must call this my
fusselbudgetporch."

For variety, you may wish to lean toward
your partner with your face close to hers
as you say this, causing her to lean a bit
backward.

A: "Yes, sir. **Whatever** you say,
sir."

B: "Now let us **both** get some
sleep for **you** have a **long** day of
work ahead of you.
And **be sure** to remember
everything I taught you."

Point your finger at the young woman as
you say "everything."

A: "I'll do my best, sir."
But to herself
the young woman thought,
"What have I gotten into?"

Say "I'll do my best sir," very politely to
him but with a worried look on your face
at the same time. Look even more worried
as you say "What have I gotten into?"

B: That very night
Mr. Fusselbudget
heard the young woman
banging loudly on his bedroom
door. He awoke in a fright
and shouted:
**"Have you lost your mind?
What's the matter now?"**

Say this very quickly and sound annoyed.

A: She replied as fast as she could:
**"Master of all Masters!
Get out of your bumper rumper
and put on your rowser bowsers.
For the white-whiskered wonder
has a spark of scorchablazintorch
on its tail, and if you don't douse
her with a puddle ruddle
of pondalorum,
your fusselbudgetporch
will soon be on
scorchablazintorch!"**

Although you want to say this very quickly, it is very important that you pronounce all the silly names very clearly so that the listeners understand you. Say this with a real sense of urgency as if you're shouting, "YOUR HOUSE IS ON FIRE!"

B: Mr. Fusselbudget **jumped** out
of bed and put on his pants,
but as he **burst** out the bedroom
door she shouted after him,

As you say "jumped," make a jumping motion with both hands. As you say "burst," make a quick motion with one hand starting from in front of your chest and going out toward the audience.

**A: "And Master of all Masters,
there's one more thing.
In plain English, I QUIT!"**

Both A and B:
And **that**
was the end
of **that.**

Say the last sentence slowly.

Finding Other Stories to Tell

The Elements of a
Good Story for Telling

Here are a few things to look for when you're searching for a story to tell.

1. A beginning that immediately captures your interest.
2. Colorful characters, but not too many characters.
3. A plot that is not too complicated.
4. It should appeal to your emotions—it might be funny, scary, exciting, or sad.
5. A strong, satisfying ending.

Try the folktale section of your library first. The stories there have many of the features listed above.

More Stories You Can Tell:
A Bibliography

These are some of the stories we've found kids most enjoy telling.

Allard, Harry. *Miss Nelson is Missing!* Boston: Houghton-Mifflin, 1977.

Baylor, Byrd. *And It Is Still That Way: Legends Told by Arizona Indian Children.* Sante Fe, NM: Trails West Publishing, 1988. ("Coyote and the Money Tree"; "Why Dogs Don't Talk Anymore")

Brown, Marc. *Arthur's Eyes.* Boston: Little, Brown, 1979.

Bruchac, Joseph. *Iroquois Stories.* Trumansburg, NY: Crossing, 1985. ("The Coming of Legends")

_____. *Turkey Brother.* Trumansburg, NY: Crossing, 1975. ("How Bear Lost His Tail")

Cecil, Laura. *Boo! Stories to Make You Jump.* New York: Greenwillow, 1990. ("The Hairy Toe")

Chorao, Kay. *The Baby's Story Book.* New York: E. P. Dutton, 1985. ("The Boy Who Turned Himself into a Peanut"; "The Hare and the Turtle"; "The Lion and the Mouse"; "The Little Red Hen"; "The Princess and the Pea"; "The Wind and the Sun")

Cowley, Joy. *Don't You Laugh at Me!* San Diego: The Wright Group, 1987.

_____. *Fast and Funny.* Auckland, New Zealand: Shortland, 1982. ("Cheer Up, Dad")

_____. *Mr. Whisper.* San Diego: The Wright Group, 1987.

_____. *Quack, Quack, Quack!* San Diego: The Wright Group, 1987.

De Paola, Tomie. *Strega Nona.* Englewood Cliffs, NJ: Prentice-Hall, 1975.

DeSpain, Pleasant. *Thirty-Three Multicultural Tales to Tell.* Little Rock, AR: August House, 1993. ("Ah Shung Catches a Ghost"; "The Colossal Pumpkin"; "Granddaughter's Sled"; "Hungry Spider"; "Medicine Wolf"; "Natural Habits"; "Old Joe and the Carpenter"; "The Princess Who Could Not Cry"; "Rabbit's Last Race")

_____. *Twenty-Two Splendid Tales to Tell, Vol. One.* Little Rock, AR: August House, 1994. ("The Alligator and the Jackal"; "The Court Jester"; "The Dancing Wolves"; "The Golden Pitcher"; "The Hungry Fox"; "The Jackal and the Tiger"; "Lindy and the Forest Giant"; "Lord Bag of Rice"; "Pandora's Box"; "The Shoemaker and the Elves"; "The Squire's Bride"; "The Three Wishes"; "The Turnip")

_____. *Twenty-Two Splendid Tales to Tell, Vol. Two.* Little Rock, AR: August House, 1994. ("The Astrologer and the Forty Thieves"; "The Baker's Dozen"; "The Burning of the Rice Fields"; "The Extraordinary Cat"; "The Giant's Bride"; "The Proud Fox"; "Red Cap and the Miser"; "Senor Coyote, the Judge"; "The Seven Stars"; "The Shoemaker's Dream"; "The Theft of a Smell"; "Three Children of Fortune")

Durell, Ann. *The Diane Goode Book of American Folk Tales and Songs*. New York: E. P. Dutton, 1989. ("Davy Crockett Meets His Match"; "The Talking Mule")

Ginsburg, Mirra. *The Lazies: Tales of the Peoples of Russia*. New York: Macmillan, 1973. ("The Bird, the Mouse, and the Sausage"; "Two Frogs"; "Who Will Row Next?")

_____. *The Strongest One of All*. New York: Greenwillow Books, 1977.

_____. *Two Greedy Bears*. New York: Macmillan, 1976.

Hamilton, Martha, and Mitch Weiss. *Children Tell Stories: A Teaching Guide*. Katonah, NY: Richard C. Owen Publishers, 1990. ("Arachne"; "The Baker's Daughter"; "The Boy Who Turned Himself Into a Peanut"; "The Brave Woman and the Flying Head"; "The Country Mouse and the City Mouse"; "Coyote and the Money Tree"; "The Dog and His Shadow"; "The Foolish Dragon"; "The Frog and the Ox"; "How Brother Rabbit Fooled Whale and Elephant"; "How the Milky Way Began"; "How the Rabbit Lost his Tail"; "How the Robin's Breast Became Red"; "The Jackal and the Lion"; "The Little House"; "Little Porridge Pot"; "The Man, the Boy, and the Donkey"; "The Miser"; "The Rat Princess"; "The Rich Man's Guest"; "The Scorpion"; "The Squire's Bride"; "The Sun and the Wind"; "The Three Goats"; "The Tortoise Who Talked Too Much")

Haviland, Virginia. *North American Legends*. New York: Collins, 1979. ("Twist-Mouth Family")

Jonsen, George. *Favorite Tales of Monsters and Trolls*. New York: Random House, 1977. ("The Stone Cheese")

Kraus, Robert. *Leo the Late Bloomer*. New York: Windmill Books, 1971.

Leach, Maria. *The Thing at the Foot of the Bed and other Scary Tales*. New York: World, 1959. ("Dark, Dark, Dark"; "Don't Ever Kick a Ghost"; "I'm in the Room!"; "The Legs"; "The Lucky Man"; "Wait Till Martin Comes")

_____. *Whistle in the Graveyard: Folktales to Chill Your Bones*. New York: Viking, 1974. ("Nobody Here But You and Me")

Lester, Julius. *The Knee-High Man and Other Tales*. New York: Dial, 1972. ("The Farmer and the Snake"; "Why Dogs Hate Cats")

Lillegard, Dee. *Sitting in My Box*. New York: E. P. Dutton, 1989.

Lobel, Arnold. *Fables*. New York: Harper & Row, 1980. ("The Bad Kangaroo"; "The Hen and the Apple Tree"; "King Lion and the Beetle")

_____. *Grasshopper on the Road*. New York: Harper & Row, 1978. ("A New House")

Marshall, James. *George and Martha*. Boston: Houghton-Mifflin, 1974. ("Split Pea Soup")

_____. *George and Martha, Tons of Fun*. Boston: Houghton-Mifflin, 1980. ("The Sweet Tooth")

Finding Other Stories to Tell

Melser, June, and Joy Cowley. *One Cold Wet Night*. Auckland, New Zealand: Shortland, 1980.

Murphy, Jill. *Peace At Last*. New York: Dial, 1980.

Oxenbury, Helen. *The Helen Oxenbury Nursery Story Book*. New York: Alfred A. Knopf, 1985. ("The Elves and the Shoemaker"; "The Gingerbread Boy"; "Goldilocks and the Three Bears"; "The Little Red Hen"; "Little Red Riding Hood")

Rockwell, Anne. *The Old Woman and Her Pig, and Ten Other Stories*. New York: Thomas Crowell, 1979. ("The Old Woman and Her Pig"; "The Travels of a Fox")

_____. *The Three Bears and 15 Other Stories*. New York: Thomas Crowell, 1975. ("The Dog and the Bone"; "The Lion and the Mouse"; "The Little Pot"; "Teeny-Tiny"; "The Three Billy Goats Gruff")

Scieszka, Jon, and Lane Smith. *The Stinky Cheese Man and Other Fairly Stupid Tales*. New York: Viking, 1992. ("The Other Frog Prince"; "The Princess and the Bowling Ball"; "The Stinky Cheese Man")

Schwartz, Alvin. *All of Our Noses Are Here and Other Noodle Tales*. New York: Harper & Row, 1985. ("All of Our Noses Are Here"; "The Best Boy in the World"; "Sam and Jane Go Camping"; "Sam's Girlfriend")

_____. *Ghosts: Ghostly Tales from Folklore*. New York: Harper Collins, 1991. ("A Little Green Bottle"; "Susie")

_____. *In a Dark, Dark Room and Other Scary Stories*. New York: Harper & Row, 1984. ("The Night It Rained"; "The Pirate")

_____. *More Scary Stories to Tell in the Dark*. New York: Harper & Row, 1984. ("The Bad News"; "The Bride"; "Cemetery Soup")

_____. *Scary Stories to Tell in the Dark*. New York: Harper & Row, 1981. ("The Viper")

_____. *There Is a Carrot in My Ear and Other Noodle Tales*. New York: Harper & Row, 1982. ("Grandpa Buys a Pumpkin Egg"; "Mr. Brown Washes His Underwear")

Slobodkina, Esphyr. *Caps for Sale*. New York: Scholastic, 1940.

Viorst, Judith. *Alexander and the Terrible, Horrible, No Good, Very Bad Day*. New York: Atheneum, 1972.

Wyndham, Lee. *Tales the People Tell in Russia*. New York: Julian Messner, 1970. ("The Woodcutter and the Water Demon")

Storytelling Resources

Listed below are sources of storytelling books, audiocassettes, and videocassettes:

August House Publishers
P.O. Box 3223
Little Rock, AR 72203
(800) 284-8784

Fulcrum Publishing
350 Indiana Street, Suite 350
Golden, CO 80401-5093
(800) 992-2908

National Storytelling Association
P.O. Box 309
Jonesborough, TN 37659
(800) 525-4514

Yellow Moon Press
P.O. Box 1316
Cambridge, MA 02238
(800) 497-4385

Guidelines for Adults to Help Kids Tell Stories

The information included here is in addition to the kids' chapter at the beginning. That chapter was meant to provide the basic how-tos of telling for kids who wish to learn stories on their own. We will not repeat, but will elaborate on what we said to them. Please read that section before this.

Our earlier book, Children Tell Stories: A Teaching Guide, *gives much more detailed information for anyone teaching storytelling in a classroom or other group situation. It also includes numerous exercises and ready-to-use handouts, techniques for helping kids develop family stories, ideas on incorporating storytelling into the curriculum, and 25 other stories for kids to tell (Katonah, NY: Richard C. Owen Publishers, 1990; call 1-800-336-5588).*

Why Children Should
Be Given the Opportunity
to Tell Stories

Children love listening to stories, and they gain many skills from doing so. When they learn to *tell* stories, the rewards are even greater. Storytelling improves expressive language skills, stimulates inventive thinking, builds listening skills, develops appreciation of other people, places, and cultures, and enhances reading and writing skills. Children experience personal growth through risk taking. They gain an increased appreciation and enjoyment of the performing arts, and learn what it means to be a good audience. Best of all, they gain a love of language and stories that is theirs forever.

Storytelling is an important life skill. When children hear and are encouraged to tell stories from an early age, they learn timing, articulation, and expression—skills they will use throughout their lives. It's hard to be successful if you're not an effective communicator, and communication is, at its most basic level, the ability to tell a story well, whether to one person or to a group.

There is, of course, a big difference between talking to a good friend about the funny thing that happened to you yesterday and getting up in front of a group to tell the same story. Once we overheard someone say, "I felt like I couldn't breathe, my heart raced, my knees shook. I thought I was going to die!" We thought he must have been telling about how he was robbed at gunpoint, but later learned that he was actually talking about the anxiety he felt when he had to give a toast at a friend's wedding! Fear of public speaking is very common. In surveys in which adults are asked to name their greatest fear, speaking in front of a group inevitably comes first. We have found that being comfortable when speaking in front of others is a feeling that comes with practice and experience.

Like many skills, public speaking is best learned at an early age. One father, who had just watched his own child and her classmates tell stories in front of parents and peers, wrote the following to our local school district office to ask that funding for storytelling continue:

Storytelling is an important activity with many long-term benefits for kids. I've noticed many young adults in business who lack even basic skills in communicating their ideas to others verbally, particularly to a group. Storytelling gives kids a real jump on acquiring these skills. In addition, it develops something that many practiced speakers lack, namely an ability to use expression and humor to captivate and motivate their audiences.

Speaking and listening skills, both of which storytelling teaches, are crucial for any profession. Yet they are never made a priority in schools in the way that writing and reading skills are. ... An added benefit is that I have rarely seen a bunch of kids so motivated to do a "school" activity. How can we lose with all these benefits and fun?

The more children are encouraged to do oral presentations while they're young, the easier it will be for them when they're older. Kids learning to ski, oblivious to the fragility of the human skeleton, tear madly down the steepest grades while cautious adult learners inch their way. Younger children are generally much more willing to take risks. One eight-year-old wrote: "I learned from telling a story that I can get up in front of people and talk. I was so scared but I said to myself 'just try' and I stuck it out. It was fun and scary at the same time. Sometimes you think you will be bad, but you are much better than you think." And a twelve-year-old said, "I learned that I really have the courage and guts I thought I wouldn't have. Everyone should get to tell stories. It will put some courage in them that they will need when they grow up."

Storytelling is one of the best ways to increase self-esteem. With the greatest risk comes the greatest sense of achievement. One sixth grader wrote: "The hardest thing I've ever done was getting up to tell my story all by myself in front of my class and all those parents that night. But it was also the best thing that ever happened in my life when everyone in the audience applauded for me. I felt so good and warm inside." That kind of confidence lingers and spills over into other aspects of life.

Storytelling, unlike some arts or sports activities, can involve *all* youngsters regardless of age or ability level. Although some people are clearly born storytellers, anyone, with a bit of hard work, can learn to tell a story well.

Guidelines for Adults to Help Kids Tell Stories

One mother of a twelve-year-old teller wrote to tell us:

> There have been few experiences in my daughter's life that have
> been as important to Dara's "sense of self" as the storytelling project
> over the last three years. She has always been shy and a bit
> awkward about making friends. She amazed us all when she told
> her story dramatically, willingly, downright enthusiastically in
> front of a classroom filled with kids and parents. But that wasn't the
> end of it. Afterward she got all of Alvin Schwartz's *Scary Stories to
> Tell in the Dark* books out of the library and devoured them. And
> this summer we went on a weekend outing with several other
> families, none of whom Dara had ever met before. At one point I
> went outside to find Dara entertaining ten other children with
> ghost stories around a campfire. Every time she finished a story,
> they begged for another. One day not long after that she said to me,
> "I like storytelling because it's a chance to act like someone you're
> not. Storytelling brought out stuff I didn't know I had in me."

Children often surprise teachers, parents, other kids, and themselves with their storytelling ability. One teacher wrote: "Storytelling is within the grasp of each child so everyone can participate and benefit. The success of kids who don't usually do well in school was surprising and especially rewarding for me, but also for the other kids." Children often gain a new kind of respect for someone they thought wasn't as capable as themselves. One child wrote: "I learned that some kids could get up and talk in front of the class like a professional, and some were kids I never would have thought could do it."

Fostering Storytelling
at Home

Stories are an integral part of family life. They have always been used to entertain, to pass on family history, to teach lessons, to initiate new members into the family and, of course, to put children to sleep at night. A storytelling tradition not only increases the amount of communication within a family but also creates a sense of community. Whether the stories told are family anecdotes such as how your ancestors came to America or folktales from various countries, they become part of the "glue" that holds a family together, defines a family, and makes it different from other families.

Reading stories aloud goes hand-in-hand with storytelling. It's a good way to begin if you're a bit timid about trying storytelling. A very helpful resource is Jim Trelease's *The Read-Aloud Handbook* (New York: Penguin Books, 1995), which includes an annotated list of more than 300 of his favorite books to read aloud.

Take this a step further and try putting the book away and telling your children some stories. You will find a whole new intimacy develops, along with the kind of enchantment that occurs around a campfire. Try to remember the stories you heard as a child. Tell any of the stories found in this book or listed in the bibliography of stories—they aren't just for kids to tell. A very useful source is Anne Pellowski's *The Family Storytelling Handbook: How to Use Stories, Anecdotes, Rhymes, Handkerchiefs, Paper, and Other Objects to Enrich Your Family Traditions* (New York: Macmillan, 1987).

Of course, you can also make up your own stories. Once you get a story started, you will find that your child will supply you with ideas whenever you get stumped. From an early age children should be encouraged to retell stories you've told them and to make up their own. Chase Collins' *Tell Me a Story: Creating Bedtime Tales Your Children Will Dream On* (Boston: Houghton-Mifflin, 1992) may be helpful in this vein.

France Moore Lappe's *What to Do After You Turn Off the TV* is full of creative ideas for enjoying family time. The author describes all sorts of activities, from simple games to storytelling to arts and crafts that can become a whole new basis for family interactions. Try turning off the television in your house for a week and see how much fun you can have. (The book, originally published by Ballantine Books in 1985, is currently out of print but available by sending $10 to: Center for Living Democracy, RR#1, Black Fox Road, Brattleboro, VT 05301. The price includes taxes and shipping.)

A rich source of stories is from your own life and from your family. Tell your children about events in your childhood such as your first day of school, scary adventures, practical jokes, vacation escapades, how your ancestors came to this country, or how your family got its name. Your children will learn about you, and they will also be discovering their heritage and building links with their past. An excellent book on the subject of family stories is *A Celebration of American Family Folklore,* edited by Stephen Zeitlin, Amy Kotkin, and Holly Baker (New York: Pantheon, 1982). (It's available from Yellow Moon Press, 1-800-497-4385.) It is full of stories that will help you trigger memories of your own family stories.

Try to make storytelling—by you and your children—a natural part of the family routine. Stories can be told at the dinner table or bedtime, during long car rides, and especially at holiday times when all the extended family gathers. The intimacy that develops as a result will give your children a strong grounding for their own lives. You could even learn a story to tell with your child such as "Oh, That's Good!, No, That's Bad!" (page 37) or "Master of All Masters" (page 138).

Storytelling in the School, Camp, or Other Group Setting

Storytelling is a great community builder for any group when done in a noncompetitive way. One teacher wrote: "Storytelling fostered a sense of 'team' in the classroom. Some students were enthusiastic from the beginning, and this feeling soon began to spread throughout the class as they listened to and enjoyed the stories. The kids pulled for each other, supported each other, and coached each other. It set the tone for the rest of the year."

Every child must choose a different story so that there is no obvious basis for comparison. If storytelling is done as a contest to pick the best, the whole dynamic will change. The kids will begin to focus on the outcome rather than enjoying the process.

Some children have such low self-esteem that they would never think it possible for them to do something such as storytelling. All they see is the great potential for public embarrassment. It will take extra effort on your part to provide those children with an environment that feels safe enough for them to take a risk. For some children it may be a great success if they tell their stories just to family members or to you. Don't feel like a failure if everyone doesn't end up telling for the whole group or for a culminating event for parents. You never know what kind of seed has been planted for growth in subsequent years. When we worked with children over a three-year period, it was amazing to see the new levels of comfort they reached with each new storytelling opportunity.

Although it's very important to offer a safe and nurturing atmosphere, make it clear that every child will be expected to tell a story in front of the group. Tell them they're not going to be great at *everything,* but it's important for them to take the risk and try to overcome their fears and inhibitions. One teacher said: "In spite of my own anxiety about the abilities of certain students, which was compounded by their reticence, I felt it was crucial to push them to do it. If we push kids to work on math in spite of their dislike or fear of it, we need to do the same with storytelling for it, too, is an important skill."

We worked in John's class for three years, and he was always one of the most creative and dramatic storytellers. The third year we happened to remark to his teacher about his abilities, and she told us that he was learning disabled and far behind most of his classmates in reading and writing ability. We were stunned, but it certainly made us aware of how all the kids have a "clean slate" when an outsider comes into a class to work with them and how refreshing that must be for them. It's very important that you try not to have expectations of who your best tellers will be—be ready for surprises.

If you have children in your group who are learning English as a second language, storytelling gives them the opportunity to understand and speak English in a pleasurable, positive way. In one classroom in which we worked, the teacher seemed a bit concerned about Melkorka, a new girl from Iceland who had barely said a word in class so far. Her parents translated an Icelandic tale into English for her to tell. When Melkorka got up to tell her story she suddenly came alive, using gestures, facial expression, and great depth of feeling. When she finished, David, the kind of kid who's not usually able to sit still for more than a minute at a time but had never moved during her whole story, burst out with "That was *good!*" Melkorka just beamed.

How to Teach Kids
to Tell Stories

Providing the Spark
to Get Things Started

One of the secrets to getting kids interested in telling stories is to make storytelling look like so much fun that they just can't wait to try it. If they see you having a good time telling a story, or a professional storyteller, or even a videotape of a storyteller, they are more likely to want to try it. Don't be intimidated by the professionals—a story does not have to be told perfectly to be successful. Children are a very forgiving audience. Even child tellers recognize this. At the end of one of our school storytelling residencies, one ten year old wrote: "I learned, while telling my story in front of my class or other classes, that they really didn't care how many mistakes I made. They just liked having me or anyone else tell them a story."

Begin the project by exposing the children to as many storytellers as is feasible. Hire professionals if possible and ask local tellers to tell stories. There may be a lot more people out there who are willing than you would ever guess. During our residency at Brookside School in Ossining, New York, *sixteen* parents volunteered to learn a story and tell it to each of the thirteen third grade classes! The children got to see many different styles of telling.

Most important, tell a story yourself. If you are confident, tell it right at the beginning of the storytelling project. If not, we recommend that you work alongside your child, or group of children, in learning a story. It will give you an idea of the difficulties they are confronting, and it will give them much more enthusiasm for storytelling.

Retelling Stories

A natural way for children to learn is by imitation. Have them retell stories they have heard you or someone else tell. Choose an old favorite or one of the stories in this book and tell it. It's important that the story not be too long or complicated.

Working With Very Young Children

If you are looking for a simple story that even very young children will enjoy retelling, try "The Dark Wood."

The Dark Wood

A traditional folktale

In a dark, dark wood was a dark, dark house,
and in that dark, dark house there was a dark, dark room,
and in that dark, dark room there was a dark, dark closet,
and in that dark, dark closet was a dark, dark shelf,
and on that dark, dark shelf was a dark, dark box,
and in that dark, dark box there was a

ghost!

Before telling, darken the room to create a little atmosphere. Tell the story to them very slowly putting in every bit of spooky expression you can muster, especially in the repetition of the eerie "dark, dark." Use simple gestures and movements to act out the scene. Look around as if you are in the middle of a creepy, dark forest, then as if you suddenly see a house, and so on. As you get near the end, lean a little closer toward the audience. Pretend to open the box very slowly and then say "ghost!" as if you were really startled.

If you are a parent telling this story at home, after you finish you can say, "Now you try it."

In a group situation, first review by asking, "What happened first?" and then "What happened next?" It's helpful to make a brief outline on the board. For nonreaders, do the outline in picture form:

Let children retell in small groups. They can tell the story in round-robin fashion or with one student serving as the narrator while others take speaking roles or even mime roles. You could also let them retell with a partner and then ask for volunteers to tell in front of the whole group.

At one school where we told stories, a number of kindergartners had gone to the first and second grades and told this story. They had a great time "scaring" the older kids, and then the first and second graders wanted to tell stories, too.

Bibliography of Stories for Young Children to Retell

Many of the "starter" and "next step" stories in this book would be good for retelling by young children. Here are some other short, simple stories.

Chorao, Kay. *The Baby's Story Book*. New York: E. P. Dutton, 1985. ("The Hare and the Turtle"; "The Princess and the Pea")

Cowley, Joy. *Mrs. Wishy-Washy*. Auckland, New Zealand: Shortland Publications, 1980.

_____. *Who Will Be My Mother*. Bothell, WA: The Wright Group, 1990.

Ginsburg, Mirra. *Three Rolls and One Doughnut: Fables from Russia*. New York: Dial, 1970. ("Two Stubborn Goats")

Hamilton, Martha, and Mitch Weiss. *Children Tell Stories: A Teaching Guide*. Katonah, NY: Richard C. Owen Publishers, 1990. ("The Boy Who Turned Himself Into a Peanut"; "The Dog and His Shadow"; "The Frog and the Ox"; "How the Rabbit Lost Its Tail"; "The Sun and the Wind"; "The Tailor")

Kent, Jack. *More Fables of Aesop*. New York: Parents Magazine Press, 1974. ("The Crow and the Pitcher"; "The Hare and the Tortoise"; "The Lion and the Mouse")

Krauss, Ruth. *The Carrot Seed*. New York: Harper & Row, 1945.

Lester, Julius. *The Knee-High Man and Other Tales*. New York: Dial, 1972. ("Why Dogs Hate Cats")

Lobel, Arnold. *Mouse Tales*. New York: Harper & Row, 1972. ("Clouds"; "The Journey"; "The Old Mouse"; "Very Tall and Very Short Mouse")

Melser, June. *Little Pig*. San Diego, CA: The Wright Group, 1990.

Melser, June, and Joy Cowley. *One Cold Wet Night*. Auckland, New Zealand: Shortland Publications, 1980.

Stevens, Bryna. *Borrowed Feathers and Other Fables*. New York: Random House, 1977. ("The Fox and the Crow"; "The Great and Little Fishes"; "The Milkmaid"; "The Stag and His Reflection")

Helping Children Choose
a Story to Tell

The stories children choose are an important component of their success as storytellers. Here are a few important points to keep in mind:

1. Stories should never be assigned, since a child's enthusiasm for a story is crucial.
2. Each child in a classroom or other group should tell a different story. The kids will be working intensely with the stories, hearing the same story again and again as they listen to other children in the group practice. They will grow tired of the stories very quickly when there are duplicates. Most important, when every child tells a different story, it avoids the problem of comparisons we mentioned earlier. Have everyone choose at least three possible stories they would like to tell. If there are conflicts, let them draw straws for a particular story.
3. Make sure the kids consider the primary audience they will be telling their stories to. For example, twelve-year-olds shouldn't choose a spine-tingling ghost story if their audience will be five- and six-year-olds. It's usually easier for older kids, who may be a little reluctant, to choose stories to tell to younger kids. This makes it easier for them to loosen up and gives them permission to be silly.
4. If you are working with a group of 25 kids, you'll want to have a selection of at least 50 stories for them to choose from. Use the stories in this book along with others suggested in the bibliography *More Stories You Can Tell* on page 145. These stories are all tried and true—we have heard them told successfully dozens of times by many different child tellers. If you choose not to work with a preselected pool of stories, have each child choose at least three or four possible stories, and then help them decide which would work best when told orally. Beware: This is a very time-consuming process. In addition, kids will often latch onto an old favorite of theirs which is not appropriate for oral telling or too difficult for them, and there will be no dissuading them.
5. When you have an extremely reluctant child, take him or her aside and help the child pick a very short and very good story that you think will fit his or her personality. For example, Arnold Lobel's "The Bad Kangaroo" from *Fables* is such a crowd pleaser that other students will beg to hear the story again and again. You can never

force a student to tell a story, but he or she will almost always come around eventually with some encouragement.

6. Few children know their own capabilities. Some children can read far beyond the level of story they can tell orally, while some poor readers are excellent storytellers. Your gentle guidance will be very helpful. It is better for a child who has difficulty learning or who is very shy to tell a five-sentence story and feel successful than to struggle with a longer, more complicated one and end up not telling it.

Helping Children Learn Stories

Before children begin to learn their stories, it's important to discuss the oral tradition and demonstrate how it works. Do a retelling exercise using a short story you know or one of the starter stories in this book. After telling the story, divide into smaller groups of four or five. Have them review the events in the story and then retell it, with each person taking a part. Continue around in a circle until the story is finished. Then have each small group (or one volunteer from it) retell the story for the larger group. As they listen to the others have them observe how each person picks up on certain things and tells the story a little differently.

It is important to convey to children that it is best not to memorize a folktale word by word. Because they are working with the written word, some students will find it difficult to do anything *but* memorize the story. They run a greater risk of being tense or "blanking" in the middle of the story if they forget one word. Others who memorize will do a marvelous job and can even sound quite spontaneous. Memorizing is not necessarily wrong; it is a useful exercise in discipline. But most children will learn much more if they tell stories in their own words, even if the telling is not as polished as it would have been had the story been memorized.

The story outline, web, or board described in the first chapter will help children make the stories their own. After giving them time to practice the story on their own, have them tell the story to a partner using only their outline or story web/board. The next time they should have the partner hold the outline and prompt them if necessary. At a certain point you will need to be firm about them not using a crutch. Tell them they will be helped if necessary, but that if they have been practicing, they know much more of the story than they think they do. This is the only way to find the parts they need to practice a bit more.

The children can soon tell the story for small groups, then larger groups, and finally to the whole group. You may then wish to "take the show on the road." *Where Children Can Tell Stories* on page 172 will give you ideas of other possible venues for telling.

You might notice that when the children have been practicing their stories for a while, they start to get tired of them. At that point they need to tell for an audience. The story may be old to them, but it will be new to the listeners. The response of the listeners will bring back the original excitement they felt when they first chose the story.

Helping Children Tell Stories

Here are a few exercises and considerations to keep in mind as you work to reinforce the techniques for telling that we covered in the chapter for kids.

Use of Voice

Expression

The voice is the most important tool of the storyteller; it must be filled with expression. When child tellers speak in a monotone, it is best to model for them how it would sound with good expression. Say some of their lines using lots of expression. Remind them that the more they're willing to put expression into their voices, the more fun they'll have, and the more enjoyable it will be for the listeners.

Exercise: To reinforce the concept that the expression you use can change the meaning of the words, say each of the feelings listed below with great expression. Tell the group that each time after you say a feeling, they should say the simple word "Oh" using whatever feeling you've said. Encourage them to use lots of expression in their voices and on their faces, and to make any movements that they think are appropriate.

How beautiful!	I'm very suspicious of that.
How disgusting!	I'm so surprised!
I'm so sorry!	How disappointing!
Look out!	That scared me!
That's not important.	Do we really have to do this?
NOW I understand!	

Exercise: To demonstrate just how important expression is, tell the beginning of a story using absolutely no expression in your voice.

Volume

You must be patient with a child who is very quiet. Sometimes, the more confident the child becomes with his or her story, the louder the child will speak. Have the child imagine that he or she is standing in a huge empty fishbowl and must speak loudly enough so that the listeners outside of the bowl can hear. Instead of interrupting while the child is telling the story to ask for more volume, have a prearranged signal, like cupping your ear. Remind quiet tellers that their vocal power comes from the diaphragm, not the throat. They should take a few deep breaths before they go up to tell a story.

Pacing

Many child tellers have a tendency to rush and mumble the ends of their sentences. Remind them that every word must be spoken clearly or their listeners may miss an important part of their stories. If the mumbling or rushing continues, tell them to pretend that everyone in the group is just learning English, so they must speak very slowly and clearly. Another tactic is to have tellers look over their stories and mark where they should pause. Help child tellers overcome the discomfort they may feel during pauses by having them count "one, two" or say "Mississippi" in their heads before speaking. It is also helpful to have a prearranged signal for slowing down that can be given from the back of the room.

Exercise: Demonstrate the effect of pausing in storytelling by giving an example from the end of "The Mysterious Box," on page 28. After you say, "The box was open!" with great excitement, pause as you do a double-take while pretending to see the contents of the box. Then say, "But can anyone guess what was in it?" Afterward, say the two sentences a second time *without* the pause. Ask the children, "Did you like it better with the pause or without? What were you thinking or imagining during the pause?"

Facial Expression

Good facial expression is an essential part of a well-told story. Emphasize that the more a teller concentrates on the expression in his or her voice, the more likely the teller will be to use good facial expression.

Exercise: Demonstrate by telling part of a story that the children have heard you tell before, this time without using your voice. This will allow them to focus on your face and body and to help them become aware of how important body language is in telling a story. You could also show part of a videotape of a storyteller with the sound turned off.

Gestures

Reinforce the idea that gestures must help listeners see pictures in their minds. Storytellers should never overshadow the story. If the audience starts to focus on the antics of the storyteller too much, they will soon lose the thread of the story. When children tell their stories they should be able to justify and explain any gesture they are using. If they cannot explain it, it should be eliminated.

Most gestures should come from the waist up. If the listeners are seated on chairs they will not be able to see the teller if he or she gets down on her hands and knees to beg. It's better to crouch down a bit to *suggest* kneeling.

If a child wanders around too much while telling his or her story, you could try putting a mark on the floor that will be the home base. For certain parts of the story, the teller may need to take a step toward or away from the audience, but will always know where to return to. If you have a teller who tries to act out *everything*, which is a rare occurrence, you might consider video-taping. Many people have no idea what they look like until they actually see themselves.

Exercise: Loosen everyone in your group up by having them do the "silent scream." This is an exercise that shows how much can be conveyed with body language. Warn everyone that they must carefully listen to *all* your directions. First, tell them at the count of three you want them to scream as loud as they can. (This direction usually elicits great excitement from the kids and horrified looks from other adults.) Tell them to pretend that an awful monster is just about to grab them. Then say, "The second part of my directions is even more important. *You must not make a single sound when you scream.* Scream with your hands, your face, with your whole upper body—and no falling on the floor!"

Eye Contact

There are two basic kinds of eye focus used during storytelling. *Direct eye-to-eye contact* is when the teller looks directly into the eyes of the listeners. This is appropriate during the introduction and any narrative parts. To reinforce the importance of this kind of eye contact, do the following exercise with kids.

Exercise: Tell them that you are going to tell part of a story using lots of good expression in your voice and on your face and including any gestures that are appropriate. However, you will *not* do something that is *very* important. When they know what it is, they should raise their hands. Then tell the beginning of a story without any eye contact. Exaggerate by looking up at the ceiling and out the window. Afterward, ask the kids how the lack of eye contact affected them. Were they as interested in the story as they are when you look at them?

Character-to-character direct eye contact is when the teller, who is pretending to be one character, looks right at the audience and talks to them as if they are another character. For example, in "The Three Billy Goats Gruff," it is very effective if the teller uses a mean, loud troll voice and says, "Who's that tripping over my bridge?" while looking right at the audience. The teller should make the listeners feel as if they are one of the Billy Goats Gruff. It's important for the teller not to focus on one person but the whole audience. This must be emphasized with kids because they tend to want to look at one person, perhaps a good friend. If the friend smiles or responds in any way, the teller will become distracted or lose concentration. Remind them that they must keep their eyes moving across the audience.

Exercise: Have a few volunteers, one at a time, come to the front of the group and try being the troll. When they say, "Who's that tripping over my bridge?" have them point their index finger and scan the audience from one side to the other. This makes *all* the listeners feel like the teller is talking right to them.

Visualization is when the storyteller pretends to "see" what's happening in the story. For example, in the beginning of the story "Fox and His Tail" on page 62, the storyteller says, "Just ahead he saw a small cave." If the storyteller "sees" the cave, it will be easier for the listeners to "see" it.

Exercise: (1) First say, "Just ahead he saw a small cave," without focusing your eyes on it. (2) Say it again; this time focus your eyes on a certain spot out toward the center of the audience as if you see the cave in front of you. Pointing with your finger will help you focus your eyes on the spot. (3) Kids will often turn sharply to the left or right to look at an imaginary object. Remind them that it's very important to always keep their faces toward the middle of the audience so that everyone can see their facial expression. Demonstrate by saying, "Just ahead he saw a small cave," again, this time looking far to one side. Point out that one side of the audience may have seen your face well, but the other saw only your back.

Introductions and Endings

If you plan to have the children in your group eventually tell their stories for parents, at a home for senior citizens, or in another classroom, have them always begin by introducing themselves to the group even if everyone knows them. It's good practice for when they eventually tell to other groups where everyone *doesn't* know them.

Endings are often initially awkward for child tellers. They must be taught to bow and then to accept the applause of their listeners graciously. Emphasize that they must say, "Thank you," before returning to their seats.

Exercise: To get child tellers used to the idea of being in front of an audience, do the following "presence" exercise just before the children begin to tell for the entire group. Have each child walk to the front of the room, and look around at the listeners. Then the child should say, "My name is ———— and I'm going to tell you the story of ———— ." As soon as a teller has finished his or her introduction, the listeners should pretend the story is over and clap. The teller should then bow, thank the listeners, and return to his or her seat.

Suggestions on Critiquing Child Tellers

When critiquing, be kind with your criticism and sensitive to the fact that telling a story, especially for the first time, is not easy for most children. Always give positive feedback first, then constructive criticism. It is vital that children are constantly being encouraged and that their best efforts, however mediocre, are supported and applauded. Prepare a list of things that you can say to even the least expressive storyteller, such as the following:

"That was a good effort!"

"You knew your story very well. I can see you've really practiced."

"You spoke very clearly. I could understand you well."

"You did a good job of keeping eye contact with the audience."

Since critiquing can be such a sensitive process, it may be best in the beginning, or even throughout the entire project, to do critiques in small groups while the rest of the larger group is involved in silent work or in other small group activities.

When a child is reluctant to take your suggestions for adding movement or expression, show the child our written suggestions and say, "This is what the experts say." Remind them of storytellers they've seen and enjoyed, and point out that it was because of their good expression and movements.

When children practice, hold their story copies so that you can help them if necessary. Don't be too quick to fill in the words—the more you fill in, the more they will look to you for help.

To keep the listeners involved, enlist their aid in critiquing. It provides a good opportunity for children to be generous with one another. But you must lay down the ground rules right from the start:

1. It's not okay to laugh at someone's telling unless it's funny.
2. Put-downs are not acceptable.
3. Whatever you say must be positive and said in a way that will help the teller the next time he or she tells the story.

After a student has shared a story with the group, begin by asking, "What's one good thing you noticed that Susan did when she told her story?" Eventually you can say, "Now what can Susan do to make her story even better?"

The Importance of Setting

You might want to put a sign outside of the room you're using that reads: "Please Do Not Disturb: Storytelling in Progress." Perhaps you can dim the lights a bit to create some atmosphere. If space allows, you can designate one part of the room to be the storytelling area. You may want to have some kind of ritual signifying that storytelling is beginning and that it's different from other activities. At the New York Public Library they always begin a storytelling session by lighting a candle. The children know they are supposed to get quiet as they are about to go to another place and time. You and the children you're working with may want to come up with your own tradition—a magic storytelling cape to wear or a storytelling stone that you touch for good luck just before you tell your story.

Teaching Audience Manners

Many childrens' audience manners are learned in front of the television where they can talk or get up and get a snack; the people on television don't notice. They need to be taught that this type of behavior is unacceptable during a live performance.

Storytelling is an excellent activity to teach basic audience manners. As the children begin to tell their stories, they learn that it is extremely difficult to keep their concentration when the audience isn't giving full attention. Here are some basic rules to outline for audience behavior:

1. When someone walks to the front of the room (or wherever your "stage" is), all listeners should become quiet and ready to listen immediately. The teller should wait until everyone is attentive before beginning.
2. Listeners should not get up during a story unless it is an emergency. Tell children that if they are late for a play, they will not be seated until after the first act because it is so disruptive to the actors and the audience.
3. Tell children they should be the kind of listeners they will want to have when they tell. That means keep your eyes on the storyteller. Don't have anything in your hands that might distract you or the listeners around you. It's rude to talk to those next to you because it makes the person up front feel that you think what they are saying isn't important.

Because it's hard to listen for long periods of time, break the stories up with a song, stretch, or other participatory activity.

Dealing With Nervousness and Stage Fright

The nervous energy a teller feels is natural; it is the body's attempt to deal with a new and exciting situation. One child wrote: "Learning the story was easy but actually getting up in front of everyone to tell it was nerve-racking. I felt like my face was burning hot. But when I realized that even the kids who were really good at telling their stories were a little scared, then I wasn't as embarrassed."

Pre-performance anxiety can motivate us to prepare well, get our energy going, and make us come across as vibrant and enthusiastic. As one fifth grader wrote: "Speaking in front of a group is not all that scary as long as you know what you're talking about. You just have to practice and practice until you know your story well."

The more you talk about the children's anxieties, the greater the chance they will feel more comfortable telling their stories. Share with them your own experiences of feeling nervous, especially when you were in front of a group. Let children tell about when they've felt nervous. Remind them that everyone in the group will be participating so that when someone gets up to tell a story, that person is facing a roomful of sympathetic listeners. This supportive atmosphere will go a long way in helping to dissipate stage fright.

Exercise: Do a visualization where the kids imagine themselves up in front of a group and doing really well and then having the listeners applaud and feeling great. Tell them to do this visualization every time just before they go up to tell a story.

Dealing With Mistakes

Let child tellers know it is only natural to stumble over a word here and there. They should correct the mistake if they think it's necessary and then go on—but they must never apologize to the audience! One girl got up to begin an evening of stories for parents and other classmates. Instead of saying, "Good evening, I'm Erica, and I'm going to tell you the story of 'Bony Legs,'" she said, "Good evening, I'm Bony Legs." She handled it so well—she just laughed as the audience laughed with her. The laughter loosened the audience up and made the whole evening better. If tellers laugh at themselves and take everything in stride, the listeners will remain relaxed and continue to enjoy the story.

The Use of Props

We never use props, not because we feel it's wrong to use them, but because they (puppets, flannel boards, and so on) provide images, thus keeping the listeners from being able to create their own pictures in their minds. Since most kids today have few chances to use their imaginations, we feel it's important to provide them with as many opportunities as possible to do so.

Because we don't use props, kids with whom we work rarely ask if they can. When they do, we are usually very hesitant to agree, partly for the above-stated reasons, as well as the fact that props are difficult to use effectively. Unless they are used well, they end up distracting from the story rather than adding to it. Also, when one child uses a prop because it works well in his or her story, it often starts a frenzy of other kids all wanting to use props, often to the detriment of their stories.

We arrived to work in one classroom where all the children, at the teacher's suggestion, had brought in props to use with their stories. A couple used them well, but to most they were a distraction from the story. We worked out a solution to the problem, an idea that would work well for any group of storytellers. We explained that the Iroquois storytellers always carried a bag full of items, each of which represented a story. The storyteller, or perhaps a child in the audience, would pick an item out of the bag. The storyteller would show the item to the listeners, put it aside, and then tell the story. The class decided to adopt the tradition. The teacher brought in an old pillowcase they made into the story bag, and every child put an item into it. When they did an evening performance of stories for the parents, they let a parent pull an item out of the bag without looking, and then that child would tell the story.

Tandem Storytelling: Telling Stories With a Partner

We tell a majority of our stories in tandem. After seeing us perform, kids often want to tell with a partner, so we have written up four stories for two tellers. What kids don't realize is that it's actually harder to tell with someone else. They need to feel quite comfortable with their partner, and the story will not begin to flow until they have practiced many times since the concept of timing is difficult for many kids to master.

If children ask to tell stories together other than the ones written up for tandem telling, make sure they first divide up the parts carefully. Be firm and ask to see their printed version, or they may try and "wing it" which won't work at all. If they are telling a story with only two characters, they may need to omit many recurrences of "he said," and "she replied," since it's obvious who's speaking once they have established which characters they are.

A word of warning: If you are planning a voluntary culminating event, it can often be very disappointing for one teller if the other decides not to come. You might want to have any tandem tellers sign an agreement beforehand so that it is very clear what is expected of them.

Where Children Can Tell Stories

The more opportunities children have to tell their stories in front of different groups, the more they will perfect their tellings and grow more comfortable and confident. Children can tell in public libraries, bookstores, senior centers, hospitals, at their place of worship, or for scout troops or local festivals. In a school situation, send them to other classrooms. Kids are usually most comfortable telling for younger children, but one school district in which we work takes a group of third graders every year to the high school to tell for an English class. The older kids are in awe of the younger ones' courage and are very respectful of them. Afterward they give the third graders a tour of the high school.

Planning a Culminating Event

A great way to end a storytelling project is to have a storytelling festival for family and friends. This gives the kids a clear goal. When telling stories for adults, some children will rise to the occasion and tell better than ever before; others will regress. Give the kids a pep talk at the beginning of the program, telling them to be sure and remember their expression, eye contact, and the other techniques you've discussed. We often tell them an anecdote about one boy named Carl who was hesitant to go up and tell his story in front of the adults. One of his friends, who had already told his story, said, "Carl, think of all the hard work you've put into your story. Come on, you can do it. Just don't look at the big people." (This always gets a big laugh from the adults.) We tell them, "Remember that those big people are just people who happen to be bigger than you. They would be nervous too if they were getting up to tell a story. They're very supportive, and they want you to do really well."

It's also important to remind kids beforehand that it's not a big deal if they make a mistake. You could say something like, "The audience doesn't know the story and they probably won't even notice. If they do, they certainly won't remember. What they *will* remember is how brave you were to get up and tell the story in the first place. You don't have to be perfect to do a good job." Saying this *beforehand* may prevent some tears when the stories are over.

Storytelling requires the total focus of the audience, especially because many of the child tellers will have quiet voices. Advance planning will help your culminating event run smoothly. Here are some things to consider:

1. One toddler running around or a baby continually rattling a rattle can ruin a whole program. When you send out invitations, make parents aware that it will be difficult for young children to listen to a full program of stories. See the sample invitation on page 174.

2. When arranging the room, leave an open space for kids to sit on the floor. Set up chairs around the edges and in the back for adults. Arrange the chairs facing away from the door so that listeners will not be distracted by anyone coming into or leaving the room.

3. At the beginning, welcome everyone. Say that the kids have worked very hard on their stories, and you want to provide them with the best possible atmosphere for telling them. Ask that audience members stay for the entire program, but if they should have to come and go for any reason to try and do it between stories out of consideration for the tellers. Remind all the child tellers, who may be a bit bored with one another's stories by now, that they should find a seat, stay there, and be the kind of audience they'll want to have when they tell. If people have brought toddlers, say something like, "We're happy to see listeners of all ages here, but if the little ones lose their attention spans, please take them out so that everyone can listen." It is much better to say these things beforehand so that no one feels singled out. Your comments will help make the evening much more pleasurable for everyone.

4. It's best to decide on the order of storytellers before the evening begins so that you won't have to continually ask for volunteers. Having an order saves a lot of time. You could ask the kids for ideas on how to decide order. One option is to pick names out of a hat. If you make the order yourself, keep in mind it's best to begin and end with a strong storyteller. Also, vary the length and type of stories—a short one following a long one, a lively one following a more serious one.

You are cordially invited to

AN EVENING OF STORIES FROM AROUND THE WORLD

Told by the Fourth Graders in Ms. Gibson's Class

Please plan to stay for the entire program which should last about one hour. Consider how difficult it is for young children to listen quietly for this length of time. We look forward to sharing this evening with you.

Thursday, March 14th 7:00 P.M.

5. Refreshments allow for a nice social time afterward in which parents can get to know each other better and congratulate the kids for a job well done. Just be sure to set the refreshments up in the *back* of the room so they will not be a distraction during the storytelling.

Using Microphones

In certain venues it is helpful if the children use microphones. This is especially desirable in a senior center. But be aware that every mike is different, and that it will be best if children have the chance to practice beforehand using the mike. For example, if they will be using a stand-up mike, they may hit it with their hands when they make a gesture. If they practice in advance, they can think of a way to adapt the gesture so as not to disturb the mike. Also, some mikes require that you speak right into them, others that you stand back a bit. If they will be using a hand-held mike, they will find that certain gestures will have to be changed because one hand must always hold the mike in front of their mouths. If you have access to a cordless or lavalier mike, those will work best because they allow freedom of movement and will not require practice before using.

Related Creative Activities

A storytelling project lends itself to many tie-ins with art, writing, social studies, and many other subjects. Here are some sample ideas to inspire you:

1. Every child has a different story filled with lots of great images. One idea would be to do a quilt—of paper or cloth—where everyone works on a central image and borders, and each child makes a square which features his or her story. For example, the central image could be a person telling stories to a group. The quilt could be displayed in the room during the culminating event.
2. Have the kids make posters advertising the culminating event and featuring *their* story. See the sample poster on page 178.
3. Affix story titles to a world map to make kids aware of where their stories come from.
4. Have kids create a 30- to 60-second radio advertisement about the culminating event that features them. Here are a couple of samples:

> Extra! Extra! Hear all about it! World-renowned storyteller Paul Daniels is coming to Washington Elementary School on December 2, at 7:00 P.M. Paul will be telling "Coyote Loves a Star." It is about a coyote who falls in love with a maiden star. Paul is so good that you will feel very dizzy when coyote gets dizzy. His expressions are very real! Paul has told stories in front of the crowned heads of Spain, Italy, and England! If you like Indian legends you'll *love* this story!

> Oh, my gosh! The famous storyteller Susan Thomas will be telling a story called "Hunter and Rainbow Woman." Everyone should be there 'cause thousands of famous people are going to be performing. She and lots of other kids will be telling stories at Brookside Elementary on February 20 at 7:00 P.M. The story is about

a hunter who shot a duck, but the arrow didn't kill it. When the duck flew away, she went to the far side of the ocean. Then the duck changed into a Giant Woman. When Susan talks as the Giant Woman she will scare you out of your seat 'cause it will seem like you are in the story. What will happen? Will the hunter be killed by the Giant Woman or will she make a trap? You'll have to find out! Susan has won eight Golden Awards. *The New York Times* says, "She has all the E's—expression, enthusiasm, exaggeration, emotion, and excitement." So come on! You don't want to miss a thing!

Good Luck With Your Storytelling Adventures

We have written this book because we feel that you and your family, and/or the kids you work with, can get a great deal of enjoyment from storytelling. We hope that you will make the effort to foster this ancient art form. We would love to hear about your experiences.

It's a Dramatic Story!!! **Dark Dark Dark** You will jump out of your skin!!! It's a Terrifying Story!!! What happens when he goes up the dark, dark stairs and in the dark, dark, room?! To find out come to Elm St. School March 18th 7:00 P.M. Only Tim knows and he will tell you then...

Appendix: Story Sources

Other versions of the stories we have retold in this book may be found in the sources listed below. Specified motifs come from Margaret Read MacDonald, *The Storyteller's Sourcebook: A Subject, Title, and Motif Index to Folklore Collections for Children* (Detroit: Gale/Neal-Schuman, 1982) and Stith Thompson, *Motif-Index of Folk-Literature* (Bloomington: Indiana University Press, 1955).

Bat Plays Ball

Told by the Creeks (Muskogees) to W. O. Tuggle in the 1880s. In *Myths of the Southeastern Indians* by John R. Swanton. (U.S. Bureau of American Ethnology, Bulletin 88, p. 23) Washington, DC: Government Printing Office, 1929.

"How Bat Won the Ball Game" from *How the People Sang the Mountains Up: How and Why Stories* by Maria Leach. New York: Viking, 1967.

"The Story of the Bat" from *Dee Brown's Folktales of the Native American Retold for Our Times* by Dee Brown. New York: Holt, 1993.

The Biggest Donkey of All

"Eight Donkeys" from *The Twelve Clever Brothers and Other Fools: Folktales From Russia* by Mirra Ginsburg. New York: J. B. Lippincott, 1979.

"Donkeys All" from *Noodlehead Stories From Around the World* by M. A. Jagendorf. New York: Vanguard, 1957.

"How Many Donkeys?" from *Once the Hodja* by Alice Geer Kelsey. New York: Longmans, Green, 1943.

"Nine Donkeys" from *The Subtleties of the Inimitable Mulla Nasrudin* by Idries Shah. New York: E. P. Dutton, 1973.

The Biggest Lie

MacDonald cites the Stith Thompson motif of this story as X905.1.1 *Lie: King owes shepherd a pot of gold. That's a lie.* A version may be found in:

"The Best Liar" from *Three Rolls and One Donut: Fables From Russia* by Mirra Ginsburg. New York: Dial, 1970.

A similar story (Stith Thompson motif X905.1.2) may be found in these sources: "The King and the Sage" from *Georgian Folk Tales* by Marjory Wardrop. London: David Nutt, 1894.

"How the Hodja Outwits the Shah Ali" from *Just One More* by Jeanne B. Hardendorff. New York: J. B. Lippincott, 1969.

The Brave but Foolish Bee

"The Lion and the Gnat" from *In Fableland* by Emma Serl. Boston: Silver Burdett, 1911.

"The Gnat and the Lion" from *Aesop's Fables* translated by V. S. Verson Jones. New York: Watts, 1968.

"The Gnat and the Lion" from *The Big Book of Animal Fables* by Margaret Green. New York: Watts, 1965.

The Bundle of Sticks

"The Bundle of Sticks" from *Aesop's Fables*. Illus. Fritz Kredel. New York: Grosset and Dunlap, 1947.

Stories in My Pocket

"The Bundle of Sticks" from *Aesop's Fables* retold by Anne Terry White. New York: Random, 1964.
"The Bundle of Sticks" from *The Fables of Aesop* selected, told anew, and their history traced by Joseph Jacobs. New York: Macmillan, 1950.

Clytie

"Clytie" from *Nature Myths and Stories for Little Children* by Flora J. Cooke. Chicago: A. Flanagan, 1895.
"The Girl Who Was Changed Into a Sunflower" from *Classic Myths* by Mary Catherine Judd. New York: Rand McNally, 1874.
"The Story of Clytie" from *Favorite Stories for the Children's Hour* by Carolyn S. Bailey. New York: Platt & Munk, 1965.

Do They Play Soccer in Heaven?

"The Bad News" from *More Scary Stories To Tell in the Dark* by Alvin Schwartz. New York: Harper & Row, 1984.

Fox and His Tail

"The Coyote and the Two Dogs" from *Picture Tales From Mexico* by Dan Storm. New York: J. B. Lippincott, 1941.
"Silly Mr. Fox" from *Just Like Me* by June Melser. Auckland, New Zealand: Shortland, 1980.
"The Coyote and the Dogs" from *Danny Kaye's Around the World Story Book* by Danny Kaye. New York: Random, 1960.

The Golden Arm

"The Golden Arm" from *English Folk and Fairy Tales* by Joseph Jacobs. New York: Putnam, n.d.
"The Golden Arm" from *The Thing at the Foot of the Bed and Other Scary Tales* by Maria Leach. Cleveland: World, 1959.
"The Golden Arm" from *Tomfoolery: Trickery and Foolery with Words* by Alvin Schwartz. New York: J. B. Lippincott, 1973.

King Midas and the Golden Touch

"The Golden Touch" from *The Wonder Book for Girls and Boys* by Nathaniel Hawthorne. Boston: Ticknor, Reed & Fields, 1852.
"King Midas and the Golden Touch" from *Favorite Stories Old and New* by Sidonie Matsner Gruenberg. Garden City, New York: Doubleday, 1955.

Master of All Masters

"Master of All Masters" from *English Folk and Fairy Tales* by Joseph Jacobs. New York: Putnam, n.d.

The Mirror That Caused Trouble

"The Bridegroom's Shopping" from *The Story Bag: A Collection of Korean Folktales* by Kim So-Un. Rutland, VT: Charles E. Tuttle, 1955.
"The Mirror That Made Trouble" from *Korean Fairy Tales* by W. E. Griffis. New York: Thomas Crowell, 1922.
The Chinese Mirror, adapted from a Korean folktale by Mirra Ginsburg. San Diego: Collier, 1988.

Appendix

The Mouse and the Sausage

"The Mouse and the Sausage" from *Stories and Storytelling* by Angela M. Keyes. New York: Appleton, 1911.

The Mysterious Box

"The Box With Something Pretty in It" from *Tales of Laughter* by Kate Douglas Wiggin and Nora Archibald Smith. New York: McClure, 1908. (MacDonald cites the geographic derivation of this story as Scandinavia.)

The Night the Moon Fell Into the Well

"Getting the Moon Back Into the Sky" from *The Man in the Moon: Sky Tales From Many Lands* by Alta Jablow. New York: Holt, Rinehart & Winston, 1969.

"The Rescue" from *Once the Hodja* by Alice Geer Kelsey. New York: Longmans, Green, 1943.

"Rescuing the Moon" from *Noodles, Nitwits and Numskulls* by Maria Leach. New York: World, 1961.

Oh, That's Good! No, That's Bad!

"Good or Bad?" from *I Saw a Rocket Walk a Mile* by Carl Withers. New York: Holt, Rinehart & Winston, 1965.

"Two Pilots Went Up" from *Tomfoolery: Trickery and Foolery With Words* collected from American folklore by Alvin Schwartz. Philadelphia: Lippincott, 1973.

"That Was Good! Or Was It!" as told by John Porcino in *Joining In: An Anthology of Audience Participation Stories and How To Tell Them.* Compiled by Teresa Miller and edited by Norma Livo. Cambridge, MA: Yellow Moon, 1988.

Charlip, Remy. *What Gook Luck! What Bad Luck!* New York: Scholastic, 1969.

On a Dark and Stormy Night

"Long Red Fingernails and Red Red Lips" from *Read for the Fun of It* by Caroline Feller Bauer. New York: H. W. Wilson, 1992.

"The Mischievous Girl and the Hideous Creature" by Beth Horner. In *Ready-To-Tell Tales* edited by David Holt and Bill Mooney. Little Rock, AR: August House, 1994.

"Caryn's Story" from *Nightmares Rising* by Carol L. Birch (audiocassette). Frostfire, P.O. Box 32, Southbury, CT 06488.

"Red Lips" from *Crazy Gibberish and Other Story Hour Stretches* by Naomi Baltuck. Hamden, CT: Linnet (Shoestring Imprint), 1993.

The Silversmith and the Rich Man

"Cunning Against Greed" from *A Treasury of Jewish Folklore* by Nathan Ausubel. New York: Crown, 1948.

"The Borrower" from *Let's Steal the Moon: Jewish Tales, Ancient and Recent* by Blanche Luria Serwer. Boston: Little, Brown, 1970.

"Shrewd Todie and Lyzer the Mizer" from *When Schlemiel Went to Warsaw* by Isaac Bashevis Singer. New York: Farrar, Straus & Giroux, 1968.

The Stonecutter

"The Stone-cutter" from *The Crimson Fairy Book* edited by Andrew Lang. London: Longmans, Green, 1903.

Stories in My Pocket

The Stonecutter: A Japanese Folktale by Gerald McDermott. New York: Viking, 1975.
"Hafiz, the Stone-Cutter" from *The Art of the Storyteller* by Marie L. Shedlock. New York: Appleton, 1915. Reprinted by Dover.

Tilly

"I'm Coming up the Stairs" from *Whistle in the Graveyard: Folktales to Chill Your Bones* by Maria Leach. New York: Viking, 1974.
"Tillie Williams" from *The Scary Story Reader* by Richard and Judy Dockrey Young. Little Rock, AR: August House, 1993.

Wait Till Whalem-Balem Comes

"Better Wait Till Martin Comes" from *The People Could Fly: American Black Folktales* told by Virginia Hamilton. New York: Knopf, 1985.
"Wait Till Martin Comes" from *The Thing at the Foot of the Bed and Other Scary Tales* by Maria Leach. New York: World, 1959.
"Wait Till Caleb Comes" from *Ghosts and Goblins: Stories for Halloween and Other Times* by Wilhelmina Harper. New York: Dutton, 1936.

Who Will Close the Door?

"The Farmer, His Wife, & the Open Door" from *Indian Nights' Entertainments* by Charles Swynnerton. London: E. Stock, 1892.
"The Stubborn Sillies" from *Once Upon a Time* by Rose Dobbs. New York: Random, 1950.
"There Are Such People" from *Noodlehead Stories from Around the World* by M. A. Jagendorf. New York: Vanguard, 1957.

Who Will Fill the House?

MacDonald cites the Stith Thompson motif of this story as H1023.2.6 *Task: House to go to son who fills it.* Versions may be found in:
"The Clever Fool" from *The Twelve Clever Brothers and Other Fools: Folktales From Russia* by Maria Ginsburg. New York: J. B. Lippincott, 1979.
"How the Sons Filled the Hut" from *Tales the People Tell in Russia* by Lee Wyndham. New York: Messner, 1970.

Why Anansi the Spider Has a Small Waist

(Ashanti) "Two Feasts for Anansi" from *The Hat-Shaking Dance and Other Tales from the Gold Coast* by Harold Courlander and Albert Kofi Prempeh. New York: Harcourt, Brace, 1957.
(Liberia/Ghana) "How Spider Got a Thin Waist" from *The Adventures of Spider: West African Folktales* retold by Joyce Cooper Arkhurst. Boston: Little, Brown, 1964.
(Bantu) "Chief Spider's Problem" from *African Folk Tales* by Jessie Alford Nunn. New York: Funk and Wagnalls, 1969.
(Liberia) "How Pakayana the Spider Got His Small Waist" from *Ride With the Sun: Folk Tales and Stories from all Countries of the United Nations* edited by Harold Courlander for the United Nations Women's Guild. New York: McGraw-Hill, 1955.

Why Crocodile Does Not Eat Hen

Crocodile and Hen by Joan M. Lexau. New York: Harper & Row, 1969.
"Why Crocodile Does Not Eat Hen" from *How the People Sang the Mountains Up: How and Why Stories* by Maria Leach. New York: Viking, 1967.
"The Crocodile and the Hen" from *Animal Stories from Africa* by Marguerite P. Dolch. Champaign, IL: Garrard, 1975.

Index

Activities to complement storytelling, 176–177

Aesop, 33, 59

Audience manners, 169

"Bat Plays Ball," 66

Baylor, Byrd, 25

"The Beautiful Dream," 25

Benefits of children telling stories, 151

Beginnings of stories, 17–18, 167

"The Biggest Donkey of All," 53

"The Biggest Lie," 50

Birch, Carol, 75

"Bracelets," 75

"The Brave but Foolish Bee," 59

Bruchac, Joseph, 44

"The Bundle of Sticks," 33

Character Voices, 14

Character Development, 10

Choosing a story; see Story Selection

"Clytie," 89

Community, how storytelling creates a sense of, 156

Community telling by students, 172

Confidence, effect of storytelling on child's, 152–153, 156

Contests, 156

Creative activities to complement storytelling, 176–177

Critiquing, 167–168

Culminating event, 172–174

"The Dark Wood," 159

"Do They Play Soccer in Heaven?," 70

Emphasis, 15

Endings of stories, 18–19, 167

English as a second language, 157

Expectations, importance of group leader's, 156–157

Experience stories; see Family and Experience stories

Expression, 12–13, 15, 163

Eye contact, 17, 165–167

Facial expression, 15, 164–165

Family and Experience stories, 155

Festivals, 172–174

"Fox and his Tail," 62

Gestures, 15–17, 165

"The Golden Arm," 93

Hodgden, Laurel, 75

Home, fostering storytelling in the, 154–155

"How Coyote Was the Moon," 44

Introductions, 17–18, 167

Invitation, sample, 174

"King Midas and the Golden Touch," 106

Learning a story
   helping children learn, 162–163
   memorization, 6–7, 162
   methods, 7–11
   ways of practicing, 10–11

"Master of All Masters," 138

Memorization, 6–7, 162

Microphones, 175

"The Mirror That Caused Trouble," 112

Mistakes, how to deal with, 170

More Stories You Can Tell: A Bibliography, 145–147

"The Mouse and the Sausage," 41

Movements; see Gestures

Munsch, Robert N., 117

"The Mysterious Box," 28

Nervous movements, 16–17

Nervousness, 169–170

"The Night the Moon Fell Into the Well," 31

"Oh" exercise, 163
"Oh, That's Good! No, That's Bad!," 37
"On a Dark and Stormy Night," 84

Pacing, 13, 164
"The Paper Bag Princess," 117
Pauses, importance of in storytelling, 13–14
Pitch, 14
Poster, sample, 178
Practice, methods of, 10–11
Props, 170–171
Public speaking, fear of, 151–152

Radio advertisements, sample, 176–177
Reluctant child tellers, dealing with, 156, 161–162, 168
Retelling stories, 158–160, 162

Scream exercise, 165
Self-esteem, 152–153, 156
Setting, 168, 173
Silence, importance of in storytelling, 13–14
"The Silversmith and the Rich Man," 97
"Skunnee Wundee and the Stone Giant," 79
Stage fright, 169–170
"The Stonecutter," 127
Storyboard, 7–9

Story Web, 9
Story Selection
    bibliography of more stories for telling, 145–147
    elements of a good story for telling, 144
    how to choose, 5
    how to help children choose stories, 161–162
Story Sources, 179–182
Storytelling resources, 148

Tandem Storytelling, 19–20, 171
Tempo in storytelling, 13, 164
"Tilly," 47

Visualization, 17, 166–167
Voice, use of, 12–15, 163–164
Volume, 13, 164

"Wait Till Whalem-Balem Comes," 132
"Who Will Close the Door?," 122
"Who Will Fill the House?," 35
"Why Anansi the Spider Has a Small Waist," 102
"Why Crocodile Does Not Eat Hen," 56
Wolkstein, Diane, 75
Written outline, 7

Young, Richard and Judy Dockrey, 79